Sparks & Serendipity

MARION DE RÉ

Copyright © 2024 Marion Thomas

Cover design by House of Orian

All rights reserved.

No part of this book may be reproduced or used in any manner without the prior written permission of the copyright owner, except for the use of brief quotations in a book review. Any use of this publication to "train" generative artificial intelligence (AI) technologies to generate text is expressly prohibited. Any unauthorized distribution or use maybe be a direct infringement of the author's rights and those responsible may be liable in law accordingly. For permission contact: marion@marionderewrites.fr

This is a work of fiction. Names, characters, businesses, places, events and incidents are either the products of the author's imagination or used in a fictitious manner. Any resemblance to actual persons, living or dead, or actual events is purely coincidental.

Paperback ISBN: 9798338378922

Ebook ASIN: B0DH79ZB7K

Free Story

How About A Free Story?

Join my newsletter and receive a free story about two work enemies who get stuck together in the archive room of the museum they work at!

What to expect:

New Orleans setting and French references
Enemies to lovers
Workplace Romance
Cinnamon roll hero

SKI, SPARKS & SERENDIPITY

Stuck together
Century-old love letters

Start Reading Now!

Reader Expectations

Heat level: Closed door, kissing only

Cursing: Mild (bible swears)

Notable tropes: Grumpy Sunshine, Jilted Bride, Small Town

Triggers: Loss of a parent in the past, abandonment by a parent in the past

Style: First person present, dual POV

Stress level: low

Ending: HEA

To my parents
Thank you for all the wonderful ski vacation!

Prologue

Ivy

I have no tears left to cry. Literally, I'm completely dried out. In case you're wondering how many tears it takes to get there, two straight days of crying should do the trick. I'm still in the same spot I've been since yesterday, curled up on my couch while looking at the mountain of wedding gifts surrounding me. Because, yes, when you get stood up the day before your wedding, people still send their gifts. The thing is, I can't even be mad at them. I know it comes from a place of love. They're probably thinking that their nicely wrapped kitchen appliances will cheer me up. I'm a glass half-full kind of girl, but come on—how can a juicer put a smile on my face after I've been thrown away like yesterday's trash by the man I love? Okay, the juicer might be a bad example. I love juices, especially fresh orange juice with our incredible Florida oranges. But a toaster? Seriously?

It's like they're not even trying.

The doorbell rings, and I immediately know who it is. There's only one person brave enough to visit the jilted bride. My sister, Hazel.

I drag myself to the front door and open it. Hazel is holding two cups of coffee, a sisterly smile on her face.

"Hey." I leave the door open and shuffle back to my spot on the couch.

"Oh, you started opening your presents," she says, trying not to trip as she follows me. Sitting down on the armchair, she hands me a cup. "And you got a silver cutlery set. Not bad."

"Take whatever you want," I mumble. "As an early wedding present, since you're getting married in less than a year now." You'd think that statement would make me cry. But nope. No tears left, remember?

Ignoring my sarcasm, she says, "Olivier and I decided to stay in town a little longer. He's at the hotel right now, but maybe later the three of us cou—"

"No," I cut in. "Don't ruin your vacation week on my account. You're supposed to whisk your Frenchie fiancé away on a tour around the state. You can't skip out on that. You guys work so much." Olivier is a high-demand chef in France. Dan and I actually went to visit them a few weeks ago.

"Ivy—"

I swallow hard. "Please, Hazel. Go back to normal, or I never will."

"You're hurt. I don't want to leave you alone like this." She puts her bag on the table, a frown pulling at her lips. "I'm so sorry this happened to you."

"I know," I say, picking at a loose thread of fabric on the couch. Not as sorry as I am, though. "How did I not see the signs? We were together for three years, and not once did I think he was still hung up on his ex."

She's at my side in an instant, comforting me with a hug. "This is not on you, Ivy! No one could have predicted this."

"Anyway, I'll be fine," I say, breaking away from the embrace and forcing a shaky smile. "Go on vacation. I feel so much better today. See? I'm not even crying anymore. Must be a good sign."

She eyes me suspiciously. "Fine. But call me, okay? If you need anything at all. We won't be far."

I nod, and this time, I give her a sincere smile. "I will."

After I see Hazel out, I perch on the edge of the couch and open all the cards that came with the gifts so I can promptly return them. Except for the juicer. I think I'm keeping that.

I'm halfway through when my phone pings in my pocket. I drag it out and see a calendar notification on my screen, *"Honeymoon in Winter Heights"* followed by a ski and a heart emoji.

My heart sinks to my stomach. With everything going on, I'd forgotten about our winter wonderland honeymoon. I was the one who insisted on it because I've always wanted to see snow. I'd actually dreamed of a snow wedding, but Dan hates the cold, so we settled on a compromise—a Christmas Eve wedding in sunny Florida and a snowy honeymoon in Colorado. Well, looks like I'm not getting either. Stupid Dan. All the activities that I had planned, learning to ski, dog sledding, cooking classes, wine tasting... Everything paid for, and it'll all go to waste. Not to mention all the cute winter outfits I ordered during Black Friday, packed and ready to go.

I begin tearing open another envelope, and then it hits me. I might not have had my Christmas wedding, but I could still have my winter vacation. I've already taken the days off, and Dan paid for the airfare, lodging, activities—everything. Why not enjoy it? He owes me at least that.

Plus, staying here in the apartment we've shared for the past year isn't going to help me move on.

Screw this. I'm going.

I need it.

1

The Favor

Zane

I hate the holiday season. Tourists everywhere, cheer lingering in the air, and Christmas carols blaring from speakers at every corner. I suck in a deep breath as I trudge down the path to my brother's house, but I can hardly taste the fresh mountain air. The invasive scent of cinnamon and mulled wine waft from the Christmas Market down the street, obstructing my nostrils. At least we've made it past Christmas. Six days to New Year's. Eight to my long-awaited tranquility. We get tourists all year round here in Winter Heights—lucky us—but nothing's worse than the Christmas season.

I bang on my brother's door, not bothering to hide my annoyance at his summoning me. Phone reception is spotty out here, so we usually talk face to face. But couldn't he come up the hill if he wanted to chat?

I hear his voice before he even opens the door.

"Hmm, I wonder who this could be." His signature sarcastic tone cuts through the hardwood door. "Do you think it's Uncle Z?" he continues to his son, Aaron.

"Open up, and you'll find out," I shout, refusing to match his tone.

"Oh yeah, that's definitely Uncle Z's barking," he says, ignoring me. Then, he swings the door open with a wide smile. "How lovely to see you, brother."

"What's up?" I mumble. I don't have time for niceties. I have a farm to run. Aaron pushes past his father's leg and hugs me tight.

I squat down and return his hug. "My man," I say, giving him a fist bump.

He lets out a giggle. "Hello, Uncle Z."

And that's when I see it. The cast on my brother's leg. "What the heck happened?" I ask, getting up slowly while Aaron tugs at my jeans to show me his new toy plane.

"Ski accident this morning. MCL tear." He steps aside to let me in. "It's minor, but I'll have to take it easy for two to three weeks."

"Uncle Z, look," Aaron says, making his plane fly.

"That's cool, buddy," I say with a big grin, my eyes following the toy before I turn to my big brother. "Crap. A busted knee? Sorry, man. And at the worst possible time."

"Yeah." He hobbles with some difficulty toward the living room and collapses onto the couch. I take a seat next to him, Aaron zooming around us. He sighs. "It's definitely not ideal, and my business is going to suffer. I got Michael, Zach, and Lea to take on most of my clients for the next two weeks. They've even offered to give me a small percentage."

Darwin is a ski instructor, so winter is when he makes the bulk of his income. He offers bike tours and guided hikes in the summer, but it's not nearly as lucrative. "Okay. Well, that's great, and it's better than having to cancel. For your reputation, I mean."

"That's actually why I called you here. I have three clients I wasn't able to hand over, since we're all pretty swamped at the moment, so—"

"No. I'm not doing it," I cut him off, crossing my arms over my chest.

His mouth falls open. "You haven't even heard what I was about to say."

"I know exactly what you were going to say. You were planning to ask me to take on those three clients, so I'm saving you the breath and saliva by telling you no."

"Zane," he says in that serious older-brother voice. "I wouldn't be asking if I wasn't desperate. I asked the entire town before I got to you." He smirks. "But I'm left with no other choice. Everyone else is busy, and as you said yourself, canceling would be terrible for my reputation."

"I have a job, you know. One that involves running a farm of twenty huskies. It's not exactly a vacation."

He gives me a pointed look. "Don't you think I know that Seth is running all the sled tours right now? I've seen him leave. I'm not blind. And when I came by yesterday, Daisy was the one welcoming visitors."

I clap my hands together. "Well, there you go. Daisy's your solution. She is here on vacation."

"When's the last time Daisy has been on a pair of skis, huh? That woman's not fit to teach anyone. She's been living in the city too long. Plus, as you said, she's here on vacation—not that *you* seem to care, since you've been having her work the past few days."

Okay. Maybe our sister has been helping a little around the farm, but she wants to stay active, and she's a social butterfly. People are her jam. Why not let her have her fun?

Not seeing a way out of this, I let out a groan. Seems like the appropriate answer. It's always tough to say no to my brother. After all, I owe him a lot.

"You're the most logical answer to my dilemma," he continues. "Besides, some human contact will do you good. When's the last time you talked to another person?"

I raise an eyebrow, glancing around exaggeratedly. "Hello?"

"Outside of the family," he says.

I shrug. "I've talked to Seth and Belinda."

"Belinda's like family, and Seth's your employee. Dude, you haven't left your farm in weeks. You stay up there with your dogs, and if your hair and beard keep growing at this rate, you'll turn into one of them soon enough."

Not exactly sure what's wrong with that. Dogs are way better company than people. They have no ill intent, they're reliable, and they're incredibly faithful.

He peers at me intensely with that big brother look I hate so much. Then, he glances at Aaron, and I know I'm screwed. It's not fair, using his situation as a single dad against me.

"Fine." I roll my eyes as I stand up, eager to get back outside. It's way too warm in here with the fire roaring. "I'll do it. When are they booked for?"

"I have two singles this afternoon—actually, the first one starts in an hour. It's their fourth and sixth lessons. And then, it's just a couple of honeymooners for the rest of the week."

"Great. Beginners?" I ask, drumming my fingers on the doorframe.

"Yup."

Turning back to face Darwin, I throw him my best fake smile. I couldn't have asked for a better combo. Madly in love and newbies. "Awesome."

Aaron lands his plane on my knee to get my attention, and I listen as he explains how special this plane is and that he calls it Buddy. Lifting off again, he starts flying it high around me.

Darwin casts me a look of appreciation. "You'll do great. Thank you, brother."

I groan again, ruffle Aaron's brown, wavy hair, and drag my feet to the corridor.

"Make me proud," Darwin calls from the living room. "And be nice."

Shutting the door behind me, I step back out into the snow. It was such a beautiful day, and my brother had to go and ruin it with his injury. Scratch that, he ruined my *week*. A honeymooning couple? What did I do to deserve that? I gag at the thought—and at the stench of the ever-flowing mix of Christmas spices in the air.

2

Aloneymoon

Ivy

Getting to Winter Heights, Colorado takes *forever*. I remember that fact being a selling point for us when we looked into different places. We wanted a secluded town so we could enjoy the frigid air in our little honeymoon ice bubble. Or at least, *I* did. I'm the one who organized the whole vacation. Dan just handed me his credit card—his signature move. If I were a hot-shot lawyer, maybe it'd be my move too, but a nurse's salary doesn't come with a bottomless checking account. With all this time on my hands in planes, trains, and taxis, I'm starting to rethink this whole aloneymoon thing.

This trip has barely started, and it's getting more excruciating by the minute. Guess who got an upgrade to business class for the flights? Yay, the lucky bride, who had to explain to the flight attendants why there wasn't a lucky husband to upgrade alongside her.

Who do you think had a limo waiting at the airport for the transport to the train station? Yup, you guessed it.

And another limo for the transfer to the ski resort? Take a wild guess. Along the way, I discovered that I still had some tears left in me.

The only upside was the unlimited champagne on board each mode of transport, so when I arrive at my beautiful chalet hotel, I don't even feel my heart breaking or the tears rolling down my cheeks as I explain, again, that I'm vacationing solo. And the pity smile of the receptionist barely registers in my brain.

Thankfully, my room is fantastic, just as beautiful as the pictures. Composed mostly of wood, it's incredibly warm and welcoming, but the best feature is surely the floor-to-ceiling window that takes up the entire wall opposite the bed. Right in front of it is a couch and an armchair with a coffee table. Better view than the TV, I'm sure.

Too bad it's dark out. But I already feel the immensity of the mountain on the other side of the glass.

Throwing the swan-shaped folded towels, rose petals, and box of chocolate on the plush carpet, I crawl into bed, my bloodshot eyes swollen from all the tears.

I hate Dan for doing this to me. Who decides to go steady with a person when they have feelings for someone else? Who gets *engaged* when they are hung up on another woman? He's the one who proposed! It's not like I pressured him into marrying me. We'd been together for three years and had barely started living together when he popped the question. I didn't expect it. I'm not sure I even wanted it. And I definitely didn't think we were there yet. Well, as it turns out, we weren't.

Getting out of bed, I pick up the heart-shaped chocolate box from the floor and the bottle of champagne chilling in an ice bucket on the coffee table and sit back on the bed.

Take notes, travel bloggers—this is how an aloneymoon begins.

The next day, my usual cheerful attitude perks up as I awaken to the glorious sun shining above those gorgeous snow-capped mountains. As I suspected, the view is outstanding. Even better than in the pictures. I hop out of bed, suddenly dying to go outside and step on the crisp snow, to feel the cold air on my face. Yes, this is exactly what I need.

After unpacking my suitcase, I take a shower and get dressed for my first day out. I'll spend the rest of the morning exploring the town, and this afternoon, I have my first-ever ski lesson followed by a relaxation session and a massage at the spa. When I was planning the trip, I figured the massage would be welcomed since neither of—*I* have never tried skiing before.

Screwing my white-and-pink beanie over my hair, I slip into the matching winter coat I bought for the occasion. I glance at myself in the mirror and approve—until I see "Mrs" embroidered in golden letters on the back. Tears spring to my eyes again, but I shake my head. It's *fine*. It's just a coat. I'm not going to let that little detail ruin my day. Or my outfit.

I skip down to the lobby and revel in how beautiful the hotel is. You feel like you're in a wood-and-gold chalet with rustic palace vibes. It's very chic with its golden chandeliers, vintage furniture, and wood-paneled walls.

After enjoying a copious continental breakfast, I step outside. Surprisingly, it's not as cold as it looks, but it's incredibly bright, which helps with my mood. The sun seems to shine stronger here than anywhere else in the world, and the rays are reverberating off the white mountain and warming my face. It's truly breathtaking. How could you ever be in a bad mood when you live here?

I walk down the street of my hotel, and I'm greeted by a charming, quaint small-town atmosphere. The street is lined with snow-covered buildings, most of them made of bricks and stone with touches of wood adding to the rustic ambiance. They're all adorned with Christmas lights, which promises an enchanting atmosphere when night falls. Most of the buildings host souvenir shops, local specialty stores, winter clothing outlets, restaurants, and hubs for winter activities. I also notice a convenience store, a salon, and a bakery-slash-café. It's a little crowded for such a small town, but with the holidays in full swing, it makes sense. Initially, I wanted to come a little later in the season, but Dan couldn't get the time off. As the thought hits, I shake my head vehemently as if to kick him out of my head.

Just as I'm about to step into a cute soap store, Hazel calls, so I sit down on the bench in front of the shop.

"Hey," I say.

"Hi there. How are you holding up?" The connection is shaky, but I can tell her tone is grave.

"Good. I'm *really* good, actually," I lie. "I'm in Colorado."

I hear a ruffle of movement from her end. "What? I can't hear you very well. What did you say?"

Well, they did warn us that the reception was spotty here on the brochure. "I'm in Colorado?"

Getting up, I start walking down the street, hoping to catch a better signal. I only hear a snippet of what she's saying, but it's enough for me to understand her disbelief.

"Yes. I went alone," I explain.

More weird disconnecting sounds hit my ear, and then nothing. I glance at the screen and see that the call has ended. I try calling her back, but it's not working anymore. So I try texting her.

> Ivy
> I'm on my honeymoon in Colorado. Cell service is crappy here. Hope you're having fun in the sun.

Minutes later, an answer comes through.

> Hazel
> I wasn't sure I was hearing you right. I'm glad you still went. It'll do you good.

> **Ivy**
> You have no idea. I'm already in love with snow! After twenty-eight years of waiting, snowflakes have not disappointed.

> **Hazel**
> Awesome! Have fun, and text me if you need anything.

I text her thanks and that I love her, but the message doesn't go through.

Stowing my phone, I top off the morning by doing some shopping and enjoying a walk in the snow. Then, I grab a light lunch in a charming little restaurant before retreating to my room. Putting my ski outfit on, I walk to the rendezvous point at the other end of the street for my ski lesson.

When I venture into the small wooden shack, the jingling bells signal my presence. It's just one large room, a high desk situated straight ahead and a waiting area on the side.

Just as I'm wondering whether there's another bell I should ring, a large man with long, bushy brown hair erupts from a back room behind the desk, startling me.

"Oh, hi!"

His dark eyes look me up and down, and a low groan escapes him.

I shift on my legs. Is he even supposed to be here? He looks like he belongs in a mountain cave, not a small ski shop. Definitely too big to be allowed—kind of like Hagrid in Harry Potter—except he's not a half-giant. He has the body of a Viking and oozes sexy, rugged charm. I didn't even know that was a thing, but here we are. He's wearing a thin sweater that defines his many, *many* muscles.

Yup. It warmed up pretty quickly in here.

Zane

I'm stuck ogling the woman before me, unable to produce any words. Probably just stunned by all the pink she's wearing. A pink-and-white jacket, pink snow pants, pink gloves, and pink boots. No need to ask her favorite color.

Taking off her—you guessed it—pink beanie, she shakes out her dark-brown hair, and her glossy locks catch the light. She has some sort of copper highlights that illuminate her face. "Um, I'm Ivy Clark. I'm here for the ski lesson."

I look at the paper Darwin left on the desk with the booking information. "I have an Ivy and Dan Ross here."

She blushes, unzipping her coat to reveal a very *pink* sweater. "Yes, well. It's just me. And it's Clark."

"The booking mentioned a honeym—"

"It's just me," she says sharply, then sways on her feet, looking around. "But you can keep the money for both."

I don't ask any more questions because I really don't want to know.

"Okay." I walk around the desk and grab the equipment Darwin rented, then motion for her to sit down on the bench.

I hand her the ski boots first. "Here. Try these on and let me know if they fit."

She stares at me for a second, then at the boots.

"Sorry," I say. "We ran out of pink."

A small smile tugs at her lips. "That's fine," she says, taking her boots off. "I probably don't need any more."

That we can agree on.

She struggles to secure the boots, so I squat down to help her. I slide both of her feet into the rigid boot shells, then start closing the various straps and buckles.

"Ah!" she screams as the first buckle latches with a loud *clack*.

A wave of panic washes over me. "Did I hurt you?"

She looks down, then shakes her wavy hair. "No, I don't think so. It just scared me."

"Scare easily, huh?" I say, moving on to the other foot.

She twists her mouth to the side. "Sorry."

I get back up. "Walk around. Tell me how it feels."

She starts walking across the room—well, "walk" might be a strong word. But in her defense, getting around with ski boots for the first time is like learning to put one foot in front of the other all over again.

"So?" I ask, one thumb tucked in my back pocket.

She adjusts the straps and takes a few more steps, wearing a confused expression.

"Well, do they fit? We got them based on your shoe size, but sometimes the model or the thickness of your socks can make a difference."

"No. I don't know," she mumbles, bending her ankle to the side to get a better look, and I can't help but roll my eyes. Thankfully, she doesn't see it.

"We're not shoe shopping here, Ivy. Just tell me if it feels okay."

She raises a perfectly plucked eyebrow when I say her name, but she doesn't comment. Good. I'm not about to call her "Mrs. Ross" or "Mrs. Clark" or whatever her name is, despite what's written on the back of her coat. I've always called people by their first name, even my teachers in high school—not that I attended long.

"I guess it's fine. Is it normal if it hurts a little here?" she asks, showing me her ankle.

"Hurts how?"

"Like it's compressed, and it can't move."

"That's kind of the point," I say with a sigh. "If it moves, you might lose the boot, or worse, break your ankle."

Her forest-green eyes widen. "Oh, okay."

"But it shouldn't hurt, either."

I squat back down and slide a finger between her ankle and the cuff of the boot. It fits snugly. "Seems fine to me. Not too loose. A little discomfort is normal in the beginning. Can you bend forward a bit?"

She does as I ask, and everything looks in order.

"Now, for the helmet."

Looking at the size of her head, I figure she's probably a Small. I hand it to her.

She grimaces, holding the helmet at arm's length. "Is that really necessary? I mean, we're not going to be doing any crazy acrobatics, right? I've never skied before. I'm pretty sure I put that down on the form."

A low chuckle rumbles out of me. "Yeah, no kidding. Helmet's mandatory. Even if we're not training for the Olympics."

She takes it from my hand a little too harshly, and I'm surprised by her attitude. I didn't think she had that in her. She slips the helmet on, and it fits. Hallelujah. We're ready to go. Grabbing the skis Darwin rented for her, I stand them next to her to check her height.

"I don't get poles?" she asks, pointing at my pair that's leaning against the wall.

"Nope. Don't need them for your first lessons. Let's go." I was two seconds away from saying, "Let's get this over with," but I caught myself just in time.

Darwin owes me big time.

3

The First Lesson

Ivy

If the guy wasn't so rude, I'd probably be all flustered around him. He's exactly my type—strong muscles, sharp jaw, and deep gray eyes. His hair is a little long and bushy, but the light-brown color takes some of the edge off. Really, he's Dan's polar opposite. But it was never Dan's looks that attracted me the most. He won me over with his nice-guy routine, saying all the right things. But grumpy mountain man? Definitely the kind of male specimen everyone is attracted to. Until you land on that resting scowl. But I shouldn't be surprised. There's always something wrong with men. Sometimes it's a sour temperament, and sometimes it's their inability to process their feelings. Or be a decent human being.

"You coming?" he asks, one eyebrow raised.

I swallow hard. "As fast as I can with these things on." I'm not sure I'll ever get used to these boots. They're clunky, heavy, and uncomfortable as hell. And they're an ugly shade of yellow, but that's beside the point.

He turns back around, and I follow him to the ski lift at the base of the mountain. He's carrying my skis on one shoulder and his own on the other, and he's managing to walk with his ski boots without looking like a disjointed puppet. He doesn't have a coat on, but he probably doesn't need it. His skin must be thick enough, and he has all that hair to keep him warm.

After what feels like an eternity, we finally reach the bottom of the lift, and I'm already sweating like a pig.

He drops the skis on the packed snow and glances at me. "Clip them on. Front first, then back."

"Um, okay." As soon as my boot touches the ski, it slides forward, and I almost do the splits, catching myself just in time.

With a long sigh, he slides it back into place, then braces his hands on the ski as I try again. I push my boot into the bindings as hard as I can, but it won't clip on. I let out a frustrated huff. "I can't."

"Hold on to me," he says, and I place my hands on his strong shoulders, resisting the urge to squeeze them. He wraps his hand around my knee, and even with the multiple layers I'm wearing, he can almost circle it with his large hand. He firmly presses my leg down, and with a loud clack, my boot hooks to the ski. Then, he walks around to my other side, and we repeat the process for the other leg.

"Thank you," I say. I try to stand without falling down, but it's super slippery, even though we're on flat ground. This is starting to look a lot more complicated than I thought.

He clips his own skis on in a nanosecond. "Have you ever taken a ski lift before?"

I arch an eyebrow.

"Never mind," he mutters, shaking his head. "Follow me."

Grunting, I try to move, but I only manage to slide a few inches. "Um, I can't." When I glance up, I realize he's already far ahead.

I wave my arms over my head and yell, "Hey, wait! I'm stuck."

Turning around, he shakes his head and glides back toward me.

My neck warms until I'm probably red as a tomato. "I can't get moving."

His shoulders drop. "You have to use your body," he says, as if it's the most obvious thing in the world. "Just push from your thighs, and help yourself with your arms. Skiing is about balance."

"Okay." I glance up at him. "By the way, what's your name?"

Frowning, he snaps his head toward me. "Why?"

What a weird way to answer a pretty basic question. "Well, so I know your name in case I need to call out to you."

He averts his eyes, then brings them back to me. "Zane. But you won't. Need to call me, that is."

"Well, this isn't working, Zane," I say, trying not to get frustrated with myself.

"It's not that difficult. Form a V shape with your skis, the tips further apart, and then push outward with your legs and use your body to help you move."

I nod and try to do as he says. I feel more like a penguin than a human right now, but it does kickstart some movement. Unfortunately, it's not enough to actually make me go somewhere.

With a groan, he slides in behind me, and I'm suddenly wrapped in his fresh mountain scent. Like pine and nature, all bottled up in the perfect aroma. He places some pressure on the middle of my back. "Now, use your legs and arms to get going."

I try to ignore the fact that a man currently has his hands pressed on my back. A man who's not my ex-fiancé. A man with large hands that seem to burn through my thick coat. He probably doesn't need a heat pack to stay warm out here. That's handy—no pun intended.

I jiggle my body, and it finally works. I'm moving. Slowly, but it's progress. Zane quickly appears at my side, then overtakes me, and I follow him to the ski lift. That was the hardest task of my life. My ski lesson literally just started, and I'm already sweating like crazy.

"Woo-hoo," I say, pumping my fist in the air when I get to the base of the lift. Hey, a positive attitude goes a long way. "I did it."

Zane arches an eyebrow. "You haven't even done anything yet," he says, totally killing my vibe.

"Hey, Shane," he greets the ski lift operator. I'm guessing he's twenty-something, though it's hard to tell with the beanie and sunglasses he's wearing. His smile, however, is as bright as the snow that blankets the slopes.

"Zane." His eyes travel from Zane to me, and I give him a small wave. "Oh, you're filling in for Darwin today?"

"This week," he says, his low voice reverberating. "Tore his MCL."

Shane winces. "Oh. That's tough."

"Tell me about it," Zane says, shaking his head. Though I'm pretty sure Shane was talking about the guy tearing his knee ligament, not the fact that Zane's stepping in for him.

"Ready?" Zane asks, turning to me.

I gaze up at the lift. "Um, nope." Then, I swing to face him. "Wait, are you even a real instructor?" I ask, a hand on my hip. That would explain a lot.

He sighs, not bothering to hide his exasperation. Behind him, Shane lets out a small laugh as Zane retracts toward me. "I'm filling in for my brother. It's his company, but I do have a ski instructor certification. Just haven't used it in a while."

"Clearly," I say. I expect a rude response, but it doesn't come.

Instead, he glances at the lift, then at me. "It'll be fine. It's just the bunny hill. You know, the training slope."

I follow his gaze to the top of the small hill. He's right. It's not high at all, and the incline is gradual. While it's a little disappointing that I won't be zipping down this breathtaking slope surrounded by gorgeous mountain terrain, it's probably for the best. This is definitely scary enough for me.

"What kind of lift is this? I've only seen the ones where you sit on a bench." And this one looks a lot more intimidating. A pole attached on a conveyor belt arrives at lightspeed. Skiers grab it, stick it between their legs, and up they go.

"It's a drag lift. We use these for smaller slopes. You'll be fine. Kids are doing it, see? It's easy." He points to a group of kids taking the lift. "You got this?" he asks. "I'll ask the operator to slow it down for you."

"Probably a good idea," I say with a small smile, and he almost responds with one of his own. Who knew he had it in him?

Shane slows down the lift, and the pole comes to a complete stop so I can secure it before he starts it up again. "Don't worry, you're going to do fine," he says as the perch yanks me up the hill. "Just hold on and don't sit down."

It looks easy enough, but what they don't tell you is that the ground is bumpy. Sure, it's covered in packed snow, so your skis *glide*, but you're pulled through a lot of rough areas that you need to be prepared for. Except I'm not, and I fall on my side about halfway up. I hold onto the perch at arm's length, letting out a squeal as it drags me up the hill.

"Drop the perch," Zane's loud voice thunders behind me, and he doesn't have to tell me twice.

"Move out of the way," he bellows, but the bulky thickness of the equipment I'm wearing, not to mention the long planks attached to my feet, make it impossible for me to move like a normal person. I stay flailing where I fell.

"Watch out," he screams, but there's no avoiding it. To keep from colliding with me, he drops his own perch, and it knocks me right in the head.

4

Sunny Has A Temper

Zane

"Ivy!" I yell, skiing up beside her before dragging her off to the side. Shane stopped the lift, but he was a few seconds too late.

"Are you okay?" I ask, sitting next to her. My heart races in my chest. It hasn't pounded like this since last summer, when I was chasing my dog Burger who ran away.

She flashes a side grin. "Now I know why the helmet is mandatory."

My tightened muscles relax. Thank heavens. The last thing I need is a client getting injured. Darwin would have my skin. "Exactly," I say, heaving out a sigh. "Come on." Standing up, and I stick my hand out to help her to her feet, then hand her the ends of my poles. "Hold on."

I hoist her up, guide her across the path of the lift, and give a thumbs-up to Shane to indicate he can start it back up.

"What now?" she asks, a hand propped on her small hip.

I blink back at her, surprised that she recovered from that fall so quickly. Sure, she wasn't injured, but it was kind of scary, especially for a first-timer. But here she is, a smile plastered on her face, ready to go.

"Well, we'll have to start the lesson from here." It's not ideal to begin in the middle of the slope, but we'll have to go down one way or another. "Rule one, always bend your knees. Your ankles should be pressed against the cuff as much as possible."

She does as I say, and surprisingly, her posture isn't too bad.

"Okay. Now, place your hands on your knees—It'll help with your balance—and try to form a V shape with your skis. That's the snowplow position."

"Like I did earlier?"

"No, the opposite. This time, the tips of your skis have to be close together, and the backs further apart. Like this."

I demonstrate the form. She tries, but being halfway down the "hill" isn't helping. Now that I think about it, Darwin probably shows them how to do the snowplow before going up. Something I should have done. But this isn't my job, after all!

She keeps trying and manages to get the ski tips close, but it's not good enough.

Sighing, I situate myself with my back to the slope, facing her. I hold my poles horizontally in front of us. "Hold onto these and let yourself slide. Try to do the snowplow as much as you can."

I start to glide back down, and she lets out a loud gasp. I glance around. "What?"

"We're going downhill, and you're not looking."

"Relax. Nothing's going to happen. And anyway, I am looking," I say, stealing a glance to see that the path is still clear. "When you ski, you have to pay attention to your environment. That's why you always look straight ahead and not at your skis."

I start sliding again, and her gaze falls to the ground. I grumble, "What did I just say?"

"But—"

"Eyes up here."

She gives me a lopsided grin, and I feel her relaxing on the other end of the poles as we glide down. She manages to hold her position, and I'm impressed at her fast learning.

"I did it!" she chirps loudly as we reach the bottom of the slope. "I skied."

A snort escapes me. "*I* skied. You slid."

She pouts. "So, what do we do now?" She looks eager to go back up again. Why? It's a mystery to me. The girl got decked by a lift perch twenty minutes ago, and she's still as excited as my dogs when they're about to pull a sled.

"We're done for today." Bending down, I free her from her skis.

Her arms drop to her sides as she takes a small step back. "Already?"

"Oh yes." I nod. "You're not ready to go up again. I think that was enough excitement for one day." As much for her as for me. I've reached my limit of human interaction for one day. She's sucking my energy. And besides, I really don't want to get her killed on the slopes.

Her shoulders slump. "But I want to learn to ski. That's why I came all the way here."

"And I'll teach you. As much as I can, anyway. I won't be turning you into a gold medalist anytime soon, but hopefully, you'll be skiing on your own on a green run by the end of the week. A blue, if we're lucky."

She places a hand on her hip, pinning me with a pointed look. "Well, can you at least show me the proper posture for skiing down? It'll be easier on flat ground."

I sigh. Though I'm eager to get back to my actual job, she has a point. "Fine. Here."

I demonstrate the different moves and positions.

"Wait, you're going too fast. I don't have time to—"

I release a growl, then repeat the moves again, this time at an excruciatingly slow pace. "Did you get everything?"

Her face falls. "I did. But you don't have to be so mean all the time, you know. It's not my fault your brother's injured and you have to teach me. I'm going through some stuff right now, and I would appreciate it if you could cut me some slack, okay?" she says, her lips wobbling.

I raise an eyebrow. "Are you going to cry?"

"Shut up," she yells, then storms away—or at least, she tries to. Every step is a struggle with ski boots when you're not used to wearing them.

She lets out a frustrated scream. "Argh!" Bending down, she unstraps her boots and whips them off. *Then*, she storms away.

What the heck is this woman doing? I hear people whispering around me, but that's the least of my concerns. She'll get frostbite if she keeps trudging through the snow in her socks. Her hotel is almost a mile away.

Taking my skis off, I hurry after her, but the heavy boots slow me down. Dammit. It really is hard to run in these stupid boots. I pick up my pace until finally, she's at arm's length. I wrap my arms around her, pick her up, and throw her over my shoulder. Even with all that ski gear on, she's light as a feather.

She releases a loud scream. "Put me down," she yells, hitting me on the back.

Looks like Sunny has a temper after all. I just growl, ignoring her as I haul her down the sidewalk to her hotel.

Once inside the lobby, I put her down.

She stumbles a couple of steps back, her flushed face boiling with rage. "I am not a toy! Why does everyone think they can just pick me up, then throw me away?"

"I didn't throw you away," I say, shaking my head. Well, I might have put her down a little harshly. I don't always feel my strength sometimes. Plus, I work with huskies all day long, and they're incredibly tough. "I just didn't want you to freeze," I add in my defense. "That's real snow on the ground, you know."

She blows out a puff of air, then crosses her arms. "Thanks for the fun fact. Now you can go."

"Gladly," I bark, turning away. But something prevents me from moving, and this time, it's not my ski boots. I actually feel *bad* for her. I know, shocking. I don't often experience empathy for other human beings. On top of that, my brother will skin me alive if I blow this. Turning back around, I lower my voice. "Look, I'm sorry, okay?" I release a sharp breath. "I lost my patience and was a bit harsh with you. It won't happen again."

Just then, a little kid scampers into the lobby with a loud giggle. He's holding the hand of who I assume to be his mother and pointing to Ivy with his free hand. "Look, Mommy. The lady doesn't have shoes on! That's bananas."

I direct my attention back to Ivy, but to my utmost surprise, she just starts laughing, hard. Her small body shakes uncontrollably with fits of laughter.

She drops her head in her hands. "Gah. I'm sorry too. I'm turning into a crazy person." Her hands fall to her sides. "This is *not* me. Let's just pretend this whole thing didn't happen, okay?"

"I don't know what you're talking about."

She opens her mouth to retort, but then it catches up with her. Cocking her head to one side, she breaks into a smile—and damn, it's so beautiful I almost lose my balance. Her grin is so big, it makes her entire face sparkle.

Darwin was right. Maybe I've been cooped up on my farm for too long.

I stuff my hands in my pockets. "I'll go get your boots. Stay *here*."

She sits down on a decadent-looking armchair and starts rubbing her feet, which I'm guessing are half-way frozen. "Trust me, I learned my lesson."

Well, at least I taught her something today. I'm not that terrible of a teacher after all.

Darwin would be proud. I think.

5

Not That Kind of Siblings

Zane

After giving Ivy her boots back, I head home, stopping by the hut to put the equipment away. A faint smile tugs at my lips as I'm closing the door. Her husband must have his hands full with her. I haven't been this tired in ages, and I have twenty Siberian huskies keeping me busy. Teaching is exhausting.

Once I'm home, I walk by the kennel to see my team. I count twelve of them, so Seth must still be out on a sled ride. After ensuring they have everything they need, I bend down for a few cuddle sessions—Buffy, Bagel, and Bear stealing most of the hugs, as always. Once I've had my dose of puppy love, I stride out of the barn and walk up to my house.

"Hey," Daisy says, sauntering toward me. Her dark-red hair is peeking out from under her white beanie. "How was your lesson?"

I let out a grunt. "I'm not sure how long I'll survive, sis."

She laughs hard, tilting her head back. "You'll be fine. You're outdoors, in your element. Just make sure they don't die on your watch and you're good."

I growl. "Anyway, Darwin is having us over for dinner."

Great. He probably wants to grill me about today's lesson. "Has Seth been gone long?"

She checks her watch. "About an hour."

I nod. "Any more tours today?"

She squints at me. "Look at you, taking interest in your business again."

"Of course I'm interested in my business. It's *mine*, Daisy." Bruce was kind enough to teach me everything he knew, and after his death, Belinda handed me the reins. This business is my greatest pride. And the only thing keeping me sane.

"Doesn't seem like it. Seth told me you haven't led a tour in months. He says you only go out alone or with Aaron."

"I *hired* him to do the trips." Why is everyone getting so worked up about this? Aren't I allowed to hire help?

"He *also* says you don't even welcome the tourists or handle any of the front-office stuff anymore. And not just because I'm here to help during my winter break."

"Seth has a big mouth that he should probably keep shut so he can focus on his job." If he wants to keep it, that is. I like the kid well enough, but he still has a thing or two to learn. Like not talking about me behind my back to my siblings.

"Even so," she continues. "I've been here five days, Zane. I have eyes. I've been working right alongside him, remember?"

I scoff, crossing my arms. "*You* asked to work. Remember?" It's not my fault she's a workaholic and needs to keep busy during her vacation. I didn't ask her to.

"Is this because of Sofia leaving?"

My body goes rigid at the sound of her name. I look at the ground, avoiding Daisy's gaze. "Don't talk to me about her."

"Well, you have to talk to someone. You've been so different." Worry flashes across her face.

"People change, Daisy," I grumble, stalking away. "Get used to it."

"But—"

I swing back around to face her. "Don't try to ease your guilt for leaving us and only coming back once a year by trying to 'fix' me or make me 'talk about my feelings.' The only thing that'll accomplish is pissing me off. We're not the kind of siblings who spill our hearts to each other."

"Exactly!" she yells. "I'm your sister. You can talk to me. And you know what? I come back as often as I can. It's not like you can't visit me either."

I shoot her a glare. "Fine. You really want to talk about our love lives?" I ask, crossing my arms. "Why don't you start by telling me why Todd isn't here."

With a grunt of frustration, she lets out a heavy sigh and stomps back into the house.

Yeah. That's what I thought.

Daisy and I both give each other some space and simmer down separately before dinnertime, and we agree not to bring up touchy subjects again. With the air cleared, she's back to being my cheery little sister, and we walk down to my brother's house for dinner. Aaron comes running as soon as we pass the threshold, and I'm pleased to know I still get the first—and longest—hug. It means a lot to me.

Besides, Daisy only comes once a year. It wouldn't be fair if she stole his attention.

Darwin made baked chicken with his signature four-cheese macaroni—my favorite. He's far from being a great cook, but as the eldest of a family with no parental supervision, he was forced to develop some cooking skills as we were growing up.

"So, how did it go today? You had the honeymooners, right?" Darwin asks, helping himself to a scoop of chopped salad.

"Actually, it was only the wife. And it went all right, I guess. I took her on the bunny hill. She won't be skiing black diamonds anytime soon, but she's not a lost cause either." I voluntarily skip the part where she fell and got hit in the head by a ski perch. I think it's better if Darwin doesn't hear about that.

My brother's eyes widen like two saucepans. "You've taken her on a slope already?"

"Well, it is a ski lesson. And I said the bunny hill."

Daisy chuckles, and I pin her with a death stare.

Darwin shakes his head like I'm the most depraved human being on the planet. "You don't take newbies on the slope for their first lesson. Not even the bunny hill. You let them get acquainted with the gear, teach them the safety rules, and show them the positions. *Then* you take them on the slope."

With a groan, I help myself to more mac and cheese.

"Don't you remember your first ski lessons?" he presses.

"Nope." At this point, I feel like I was born with skis attached to my feet.

"Relax, Darwin," Daisy says softly. "I'm sure he did great."

Her way of trying to smooth out even more the tension between us, I'm sure.

"You didn't give her poles, I hope?" he continues.

"Of course not. I'm not a total moron."

"Glad we ruled that out," he says, rolling his eyes before he lowers his voice. "Look, I'm grateful for your help, I am."

I guess the daggers I was throwing at him from my blazing eyes finally landed.

"Just take it easy, okay? The last thing I need is to be hit with a lawsuit because someone got hurt."

I clamp my mouth shut, focusing on my food. I guess it was a good thing I didn't say anything about the ski lift incident.

6

Breaking Point

Ivy

I was right to assume a spa session would be needed after my ski lesson. It should be mandatory and come with the package or something. Maybe I should suggest the idea to Zane. The thought alone makes me laugh and cringe at the same time. He's not exactly the kind of guy you pitch suggestions to. He's the one who rips all your dreams apart, at least the dream I had of being able to ski by the end of the week.

I release a frustrated growl. He's so infuriating, with his eyes as dark as a brooding storm and his no-nonsense attitude. I just had to have a cloud over my vacation, didn't I? Something had to go the wrong way. And now, here I am paired with the grumpiest teacher in Winter Heights.

You know, I'm a nice girl. A good person. I never fail to round up my total at the cashier, even if it means pretty much adding an extra dollar. I'm the perfect target for donation seekers in the street, and even if it's the fifth time I get stopped that same day, I always take five minutes of my time and help however I can. Because I care about people. Because I'm *nice*.

So, what did I do to deserve this? My fiancé leaving me. Being paired up with a mean, gloomy teacher. Is there no karma in the universe? No 'what goes around comes around'?

I sit down on the armchair in my hotel room and proceed to pull off my ski boots. Grumpy insisted I put them back on to walk back to my room, even though the hotel is perfectly warm. A cry of pain escapes me as I release my first foot from the buckle's pressure. My heels are both blistered, and my ankles feel like they've been ground to the bone. Who am I kidding? This *entire trip* is a cloud. The ultimate storm. The one that leaves you stranded in the middle of the night with no hope of finding light again.

That's where I am right now. Removing my tight ski boots delivers a mix of excruciating pain and pleasure. Kind of like looking at Zane's dreamy face, then hearing him talk, except the other way around.

I massage my feet for a minute, and I'm two steps away from crying as I hobble to the bathroom. I'm in desperate need of a quick shower before going to the spa.

The shower helps a little with both my mood and the physical pain, and now, I'm really looking forward to the spa. A long, relaxing treatment is exactly what I need. Slipping my robe and plush slippers on, I head down to the spa. It's decorated with a mix of rustic wood and stone, giving the place a cozy atmosphere. The low lighting cast by several fireplaces adds to the warm vibes.

"Hi," I greet the attendant. "I'm Ivy Clark from room 528. I have an appointment for a full-body massage at five."

She greets me, then looks at her screen, a frown pulling at her lips. Here we go.

"I have a couple's massage under the name Ross for a honeymoon?"

"Yes. Well, um. There's been a change of plans."

Her forehead wrinkles. "Will he be joining you later?"

"No, he won't." Why do they always push for more details? Can't they just accept the fact that the "mister" is not here? *I* have, and I'm the one who was supposed to marry him.

"Oh, okay." She lifts her eyes to meet mine, and my eyes must be telling another story, because pity sweeps over her face. "*Oh.* I see. I mean, I'm sorry. I'll exchange it for a single massage. Let me know if there's anything I can do."

Here, I thought six times would be the charm, and it wouldn't hurt like heck anymore. Guess I was wrong about that.

"Here are your towels. Feel free to use the facilities before and after your massage." She goes on to tell me about the different equipment they have and repeats twice that I can come to her for anything. Anything, huh? Does she have a perfect husband up her sleeve or something?

I start my spa session with a relaxing swim in a warm pool, and it melts away some of the physical pain. Next, I go into the sauna before sipping some tea. It's not so bad after all, being here alone. In a way, I'm already used to it. Dan was never a fan of places like this. He'd come with me, but he'd be on his phone constantly, annoyance oozing out of him as he sat hunched on a chair answering work emails. If he was here, I'd have to put on my extra-happy face, show him all the cool features this spa boasts and how fully relaxed we'd be afterwards. Only, that would never happen because of his rotten attitude and inability to suck it up for a few hours. God forbid we do something *I* enjoy for once. All those times, I should have just gone alone. *I'm* glad to be here by myself today. Better to be alone than in bad company.

When the time of my appointment comes around, I pad over to the designated waiting room, and two masseuses greet me with bright smiles. They glance around the waiting room at the same time I do. There's no one else here. Looks like the spa receptionist was more focused on asking what she could do instead of actually *doing* the one thing she should have. Heat washes over me, and I suddenly need some fresh air. Like, a lot of it.

"Mr. and Mrs. Ross?" one of them ventures, looking at me with confusion.

I feign ignorance as best I can. "No."

They look at each other, then go back behind the door they came from.

Humiliation.

That's what I'm feeling right now. I've reached an all-time low, refusing a massage I clearly need because I can't bring myself to explain, yet another time, that I'm alone on this stupid honeymoon. Getting up, I hurry out of the spa, throw my towels in the designated bin, and keep my head down as I pass the reception desk—thankfully, a couple is standing in front of it. Back in my room, I fall onto the bed and scream into my pillow as tears flow out of my eyes in uncontrollable streams. How many more times is my heart going to break over him? Isn't a million times enough already? I hate him for making me feel this way, all empty, and broken, and lost. And I hate myself for not being able to enjoy a simple solo vacation. Coming to Winter Heights was a bad idea.

"Ugh!" I growl, hitting my fist on the fluffy pillow. It's surprisingly cathartic, so I do it again, and again, and again. Until I'm in full wrestling mode with a harmless pillow. I must look like a maniac right now, but I don't care. The best thing about having a breakdown when you're alone on your honeymoon? No one is there to judge.

I give the pillow one last punch, and as I dry my tears with my sleeve, I catch a glimpse of the view through the large window. The sun is hanging low, casting a golden blanket of light on the mountain that makes the slopes shine. I relax my shoulders, releasing the breath from my lungs. *That's* why I came here. To finally see snow and get some fresh air. So that's what I'm going to do.

Instead of grappling with my bedding, I decide to put my pent-up energy to good use. I gear up, shedding a few more tears when slipping on the devil boots, then ask someone at reception if they can lend me a pair of skis. Even if most of my body hurts, it's better than the alternative—having a couple's massage minus the "couple" part. Physical pain chases away the emotional ache. Besides, skiing is one of the things I was most looking forward to on this trip, so I need to get better. I'm usually a fast learner. And I really don't want to endure Zane's sighs and exasperated looks again.

I walk to the training slope, but the lift just closed, and the area is empty. It doesn't matter. I just need to put these darn things on and move, so that's what I do. I fight with my skis for hours, first to put them on, then to scoot forward a few inches. I fall a lot—yes, it is possible to fall even if you're barely moving—and unload my anger by slamming my fist in the snow and raging at my incompetence.

Eventually, I get better and manage to hold the snowplow position—I think—and even manage to skate the entire base of the training slope, until I literally collapse from exhaustion. I stay right there, lying in the snow and gazing at the dark sky with its thousands of twinkling stars.

I did it. I can't wait to see the surprised look on Zane's face when he sees that I'm not completely useless after all. A tingle of comfort envelops me as I think about him. Odd, I know. He's not exactly a ray of sunshine. But he's the only person who didn't ask about Dan.

7

Surprise

Zane

After breakfast, I spend some quality time with my dogs, then drag myself down to the ski hut. Ivy is already standing in front of it in all of her pinkness, waiting for me. Surprisingly, the sight isn't as unpleasant as I thought it would be. My eyes must be adjusting to all the colors. I look around, but I don't see anyone else. Still no husband today. Maybe he's sick or something.

"Morning," I grumble, using my boot to sweep away the snow in front of the shack so I can open the door.

"Good morning," she says with a bright smile. "Beautiful day, isn't it?"

I glance back at her but don't say a word. Instead, I stomp inside, grab the equipment, and come back out.

I can tell she wants to chat during the walk to the bunny hill because she keeps glancing at me, but she doesn't engage in conversation. I feel a little bad for her. She's on vacation, eager to learn to ski, and she's stuck with me. Probably not what she pictured when she was planning her romantic getaway for her and her man.

Once we reach the bottom of the slope, I drop her skis on the packed snow and kneel down to help her put them on, but to my utmost surprise, she manages to do it herself before I even touch her boot.

With a frown, I stand back up. "Okay. We'll start by doing some walking with the skis—here, on flat ground. Then, when you feel ready, we'll try the slope again."

"I'm ready," she says with a nod, offering a full-fledged smile.

I hold back a sneer. "I'll be the judge of that. See that pole over there?" I point to a light pole about forty feet away. "Using your body and legs, do the reverse V I showed you yesterday, and skate to the pole and back."

She gives me a firm nod, and I'm impressed by her confidence. A far cry from yesterday.

She gets going, and I can't fight the faint smile tugging at my lips. This girl is full of surprises, isn't she? Yesterday, she could barely stand, and now she's actually doing *good*. Not great—I can tell she's really struggling, and she falls a few times—but it's a huge improvement.

"So, how did I do?" she asks when she returns, slightly out of breath.

"Better than yesterday. Not that the bar was very high."

Her mouth opens slightly, then clamps shut. "Well, a student can only be as good as their teacher."

I smirk. "Then you'll be excellent. Come on. Let's go to the lift."

Once there, I greet Shane and ask him again to slow the lift for her, but this time, I go first. "This way you can watch *your teacher*," I say, and she gives me a forced smile.

She manages to take the perch without falling, so I give her a few claps of encouragement once she reaches the top. But she doesn't seem to appreciate the gesture and glares at me instead. She still looks just as beautiful with that annoyed scowl, though the elated smile she usually wears wins. No debate.

I show her the snowplow one more time, and she surprises me *again*. She follows me all the way down the slope, keeping the right posture and managing the turns as I demonstrate them. Either she became amazing overnight, or I *am* a better teacher than I thought. I guess the mood helps too.

Two hours later, we're taking off our skis at the bottom of the slope, and she looks like she's about to pass out.

"So," I begin. "Are you the kind of girl who performs well at everything and can't endure failure?"

She raises her head, her cheeks slightly flushed from exhaustion. More pink. "Huh?"

"You clearly trained on your own after our last lesson," I say, my tone accusatory.

Her blush deepens. "So?"

I knew it. "So, you *are* that kind of girl, then? But I'm telling you, skiing for the first time at your age is hard. You have to be prepared to fail—"

"Are you calling me old?" She props a hand on her waist.

Well, looks like my inspirational speech was a bust. I shake my head, rolling my eyes. "We're probably around the same age." Late twenties to early thirties, I'm guessing. "I'm just saying. Don't wear yourself out by training non-stop after our lessons. It won't do you any good. Learning as an adult is hard."

She shrugs. "I didn't have anything better to do last night, that's all."

I raise my eyebrows. Ouch. That's some honeymoon. "By the way, will your husband be joining us this week?

Otherwise, I can just return his skis." My tone surprises me. I was going for a neutral question, but somehow, a hint of annoyance worked its way in.

Her face flashes from annoyed to hurt. "There is no husband. Don't you get that? He *dumped* me. Yes, you heard me right. I'm the pathetic girl who's on her honeymoon alone. So leave me alone, okay?"

I open my mouth to apologize, but she turns around and marches away from me—with her boots on this time.

Ivy

Here, I thought Zane was just being thoughtful, not asking about my missing husband, when in reality, he just didn't have a clue what was happening. Every other person I've talked to immediately understood that my fiancé dumped me, but not Zane. I can't decide if it's a good thing or a bad thing.

With the ski hill behind me, I realize that I'm starving and hope to fill up for lunch. I had a reservation at a nice restaurant last night, but I couldn't handle another pity look—not to mention my entire body hurt. So instead, I grabbed some snacks from the lobby and ate them while relaxing my sore muscles in the bathtub. Hey, don't judge. I'm on vacation.

I walk up to my room as fast as I can with my blistered feet, take a quick shower, and get changed before walking down the narrow street until I find a small restaurant with empty tables. I order a burger, connect to the wi-fi, and reply to Hazel's text while I wait.

Ivy
> Yes. Everything's fine. I had my second ski lesson today!

I add the exclamation point to convey my excitement because, even if it's non-existent right now, I need her to believe I'm okay.

Hazel
> Oh, fun! Is it hard?

Ivy
> Very. Especially when you start out as an adult.

Hazel
> Do you have a hot instructor?

Ivy
> I have a grumpy instructor. Think, the yeti meets Garfield with the Grinch's attitude.

Had would be a more suitable term. I'm not doing any more lessons with that guy.

Hazel

> Oh . . . Okay. But is he hot?

Placing the phone on the table, I cross my arms over my chest. I'm not dignifying that with an answer. What kind of question is that, anyway? Why does she even care? His looks are completely irrelevant to the situation. What is relevant is that he's rude and insensitive, not that his eyes are fifty shades of gray or that his body is one of a Viking.

My thoughts are interrupted by the waiter, who arrives with my order, and I devour my burger in no time. Turns out, skiing really works up an appetite. At least I made it down the training slope this time, so it's not a total failure. Tomorrow, I'll see if another instructor is available to teach me. Hopefully, one that doesn't have "Abrasive" as his middle name.

After lunch, I make my way to the husky farm. It's a little out of the way, but the town is so small, it takes me only twenty minutes to reach it. The farm is bigger than I expected, set on a large piece of land with two wooden buildings that stand tall. In front of the smaller structure is a large enclosure with dogs scampering and fooling around in the snow. My heart melts in a puddle of puppy love. They're adorable.

"Hey there!" A boy with dark hair and a warm smile says. He can't be a day over twenty. "Welcome."

"Hello. I'm Ivy Clark. I have a reservation for a sled ride today, but it might be under 'Ross.' There will be only one person doing the ride." I blurt my explanation in one go and end up a little out of breath. At least now, he won't ask.

One of his eyebrows arches. Great. He clearly thinks I'm a lunatic. Well, at least crazy is better than pathetic.

"Awesome," he says, clapping his hands. "I'm Seth. I'll be your guide today. I just have a couple of things to finish up, and then I'm all yours."

"Sorry. I know I'm a little early. I was excited to see the puppies."

He chuckles. "No problem. Feel free to go over there and say hello. Just don't feed them anything."

I nod. "Great. Thanks."

I have to force myself to walk and not run to the enclosure, and as soon as I get closer, the huskies all run toward the fence and press their faces between the bars, asking for cuddles. They're the cutest things. Beautiful, fluffy fur and huge eyes. They jump at me, panting, and it's almost like they're smiling at me. In the five minutes I've been here, they've been a better comfort than anything else. Dog therapy really is a thing.

Just when I'm trying to extricate myself from a dog that's giving me a French kiss all over the face, I hear a low groan behind me. I don't need to turn around to know who it belongs to.

"What are you doing here?" he growls.

8

Lesson In Mushing

Zane

I spotted her from Belinda's porch as I was walking out the door, and my heart stopped. She's pretty hard to miss with that flashy "Mrs." jacket she wears. Why would she even wear it if there's no "Mr."? And why would anyone leave this woman? That's an even bigger question.

"I could ask you the same," she says, standing up and turning around with a hand on her hip as Bobby stands up on his hind legs, trying to kiss her. "Are you following me?"

I raise an eyebrow, and she moves aside to escape the over-enthusiastic dog. "Bobby. Down," I say, and he sits down calmly.

Ivy looks between me and the dog, wearing a confused expression. "Wait. Are you . . . ? Do you work here?"

"Yes, I work here. It's my farm, actually."

She closes her eyes for a second. And when she opens them, they're wider than ever, giving me a chance to appreciate the many hues of green they feature.

"Are you here for a sled ride?" I ask. It's the only plausible explanation. She didn't know I worked here, so she couldn't have chased me down to shout at me or kick me in the shin—which was my first thought when I saw her here.

"I am." She turns back around to cuddle Bobby, who's back at it. "With Seth."

"Actually, I'm doing the ride today. Seth is busy with something else." The words tumble out without warning.

She turns around again, frowning. "But he said—"

"And I'm saying otherwise."

"Fine," she snaps, crossing her arms.

I start making my way back to the house when I hear her mumble behind me, "I guess you'll suck the fun out of that too."

I stop in my tracks and wheel around. "What did you just say?"

Her cheeks flush. "Nothing."

I want to retort, but my gut tells me not to push it. She was two steps away from crying after our lesson this morning, and I can't handle crying. Or emotions. "I'll be right back."

As I start moving again, Seth appears with the blanket, and I stick my hand out to stop him. "I'll take over. Tell Belinda I won't be going with her to the market after all."

He looks at Ivy, then at me. "Are you sure? I'm—"

I throw him a look that leaves no room for argument, and he walks back to the house.

"Who's Belinda?" Ivy mutters behind me. "Your girlfriend?"

That rips a laugh out of my chest. I turn around to meet her gaze, which is almost defiant.

"No," I say. "She's my . . . She's . . ." I clear my throat. "Never mind, she's not my girlfriend. Let's—"

"Oh, I'm sensing a vibe," she teases. And if it wasn't so ridiculous, I'd be annoyed right now.

Another chuckle slips out. "There is absolutely *no* vibe. Now, I'm not saying Belinda is old—learned my lesson." I smirk. "But I'm not into dating sixty-five-year-old women."

"Oh!" Ivy's eyes widen, and her cheeks tint pink to match her outfit.

"She's my neighbor," I say, nodding toward the house across the street. In truth, she's way more than that. Belinda and her late husband, Bruce, pretty much raised me and my siblings. But Ivy doesn't need to know that.

"Gotcha."

"All right. So, I'll give you a crash course on mushing, and then we'll go." I jerk my chin, gesturing for her to follow me inside the barn. Once there, I introduce her to the entire gang.

"Whoa. How many are there?" she asks as we walk down the length of the barn, the dogs scrambling toward her and jumping at the wooden fence.

"Twenty. Twelve males and eight females."

She reads the names on the signs. "All their names start with B. Is there a reason for that?"

"It's a tradition the previous owner started because his and his wife's names started with B," I say, shooting her a small smile. "So I kept it up."

"Oh, that's cute. How old are they?" she asks, patting Bella and Burger simultaneously.

"The oldest is almost eleven. Buck, over there." I point to the far corner where he's lazily gazing at us. "And the youngest is two years old." I scan the barn for her. "There she is. Buffy."

Ivy lets out a giggle. "As in the vampire slayer."

I shake my head. "Everyone always says that."

"Well . . . it's the name of the show, and it was pretty popular in the nineties."

I shrug. "I don't watch TV."

She returns to petting Burger's and Bella's heads. "At what age do they stop pulling the sled?"

"They usually retire at around eight to ten years old, but it's the dog that makes the decision, not us. Buck still asks to go on rides, though for him, we keep them short. I never force any of the dogs to go out, but as long as they want to go, they are welcome to. I like to keep them around. They're a great help when it comes to teaching the youngsters."

A flash of horror crosses her face. "What happens to them after they retire?"

I roll my eyes, shaking my head. "Don't worry, I'm not eating husky for breakfast."

She gives me a pointed look.

"We have a rehoming program. Actually, Belinda has one of my former wheel dogs, Boomer, and I'm pretty sure she's going to take Buck when he decides to retire."

"Oh, that's nice. At least they don't move far."

I scratch my beard. "Yeah. A few of them are here in town, actually."

"So, what's a wheel dog?" she asks, her forehead wrinkling.

"Mushing is a team sport. Each dog has a specific place in the line and a unique function within the pack. Wheel dogs are hitched directly in front of the sled. They're the strongest and calmest." I point to all my wheel dogs. "You've got Buck over there, then Bea, Blue, Burger, and Bear."

"Okay." She nods, locating them in the barn.

"Next, we have the team dogs. They're the horsepower of the lot. Bobby is a team dog, and so are Bolt, Buzz, Bella, and Blaze. Then, you've got the swing dogs, Brownie, Buffy, Bluebell, Buddy, and Bagel. They set the pace and turn the whole team. And finally, the lead dogs. They're the ones answering to the musher's commands and steering the team. My lead dogs are Bean, Boots, Bonnie, Birdie, and Bandit."

"Whoa, okay. That's a pretty complex system."

"It is. But Siberian huskies are born for this, and they naturally learn and understand the hierarchy of the pack. I'm not saying training isn't a big part of the job—it definitely is—but the learning curve is easier than it would be with other dogs." That fact has always impressed me, from the first time Bruce explained the mechanics. Plus, teaching dogs is a lot easier than teaching people. But that's just my opinion after my short teaching experience.

Ivy's eyes are gleaming with fascination as she looks around the barn. "How fast can they run?"

"They run at fifteen to eighteen miles per hour for about twenty-five miles, then their speed starts to drop."

"Impressive."

"They are," I say, giving Bella a scratch on the head before glancing at Ivy again. "Are we ready to go?"

"Yes." Her sparkling eyes stretch wide with excitement. "Who are we taking?"

"I don't know. Who wants to go on a ride?" I ask the dogs, and all of them except for Buck and Blue jump for joy. I chuckle at their enthusiasm, and Ivy giggles, petting them all. As she does, I have a hard time tearing my eyes away. Her interest in mushing, how happy she looks scratching their ears—it almost feels like she belongs here.

9

A Good Teacher

Ivy

Just as we're about to leave the barn, a good-looking girl strides in. "Hey, where are you going?" she asks Zane.

"Sled ride," he mumbles.

Her eyebrows shoot to the roof, and her deep gray eyes travel between me and Zane, almost suspiciously. Of course. *She's* the girlfriend. That makes more sense. As the thought crosses my mind, she sticks her hand out to me. "I'm Daisy Harden, Zane's sister."

"Oh, hi." I wear a smile, trying to hide my surprise. I guess she's *not* the girlfriend. Why do I care so much who his girlfriend is? Come to think of it, he probably doesn't even have one, given the attitude he carries around. Not that everyone needs someone in their life. I intend to stay happily single for a while. "Nice to meet you."

She tilts her head to the side. "Same." Then, she directs her attention to Zane, who's watching our interaction like he's seeing a ghost. "Seth took Burger, Blue, Buffy, Bluebell, Bolt, Bella, Bean, and Bonnie this morning. I thought you should know, since you haven't been sledding in *so* long."

He shoots her a glare but doesn't say anything as he exits the barn. There's definitely a weird vibe here.

"Have fun," Daisy calls out behind us. I offer her a polite smile as I follow Zane out. He places the blanket Seth gave him earlier on a wooden sled that's parked on the side of the barn, then picks up some harnesses and walks into the yard. I watch as he calls his dogs, then pets them as they scamper toward him, a genuine smile on his face, and it's the most comforting thing I've experienced in days. If even a rugged guy like Zane isn't immune to puppy love, there's still hope left in this world.

"Can I help?" I ask, unsure what to do with myself.

He throws me a look. "No. Just wait a second. I'll get them in line, and then we can go."

He selects the dogs and harnesses them on the line that runs in front of the sled, calming them down with simple voice commands as they jump around with palpable excitement. Zane is so different than he was during ski lessons. He's relaxed, passionate, and—dare I say it—nice. Maybe I judged him too harshly on the slope. It's not his natural environment, after all. This is.

A few minutes later, we're ready to go.

"You can sit in the sled," he says, sticking his hand out to me. When I take it, a tingle courses through my arm, and I wonder how that's even possible given that I'm wearing gloves. He looks at me for a second, and I know he felt it too. With a frown, he turns and walks back toward a small shack before coming back with what looks like a heavy bag. He places it at the end of the sled by my feet and straps it tightly.

"What's that?"

"Weight bag. Since you're alone, it adds more weight to stabilize the sled," he explains while placing the comfy blanket over me.

"Oh . . ." So, this is what I'm reduced to. Dog sledding with a weight bag for a companion on my honeymoon. My *aloneymoon*.

"Sorry." He scratches his beard, glancing around. "I didn't . . . It's not—I'm not implying anything. It's just a safety issue, okay?"

I nod and offer him a faint smile. I get it, and I know he didn't mean for it to come across as anything else.

"All right, you ready? Just stay seated at all times and enjoy the ride."

"Yes, okay. Don't go too fast." I release a nervous chuckle.

"Don't worry. I won't." And I know it's weird, but I just have the feeling I can trust him. An hour ago, I didn't want anything to do with this man, but here, in this moment, I know I'm safe. Zane is confident, at ease, and that's incredibly reassuring.

He steps onto the runners of the sled behind me, and I focus my eyes forward, on the excited puppies who look eager to go. "Hike!" Zane bellows, and off we go.

The ride is everything I dreamed of and more. We pass through snow-covered forest trails and down hills, sliding across untouched areas where the sparkling snow is so thick, it doesn't even look real. It's so serene. Way more relaxing than the spa, even if it's a tad colder. I can't glimpse Zane unless I completely tilt my head back, and I don't want to be weird, but I imagine he's looking and feeling as breezy as me right now. For the first time during this trip,

I actually feel *good*. How lucky am I to be here, gorging on these amazing views and breathing in the purest air I've breathed in years?

Butterflies swarm in my belly as we sled down a steeper slope, turning sharply at the end, and it's better than riding a theme park roller coaster. I savor every second of the freeing sensation, though my favorite part is when we snake through the forest between mighty stands of snow-capped trees. I feel like I'm the star of an adventure movie—or Santa Claus.

Too soon, it's time to head back, and a pang of disappointment hits me when I glimpse the outline of the farm taking shape on the horizon. I could have kept going forever, but that wouldn't be fair to the dogs.

"Whoa!" Zane barks his command, and we slide to a stop in the yard. Seconds later, he extends his hand to my right, helping me out of the sled. His cheeks are flushed, and the expression in his eyes is similar to that of a kid on Christmas morning. Pure joy, satisfaction, and excitement. We're so close now, my hand still in his. I don't dare move because it's such a treat seeing him like this. And for the first time, I notice shades of blue dancing in his gray irises. Magnetic.

Dropping my hand, he takes a step back. "Did you enjoy the ride?"

"Yes, I loved it. Thank you so much for taking me."

"Ah, you're back," Seth calls out to him with a bright smile. "Daisy went to the market with Belinda. Do you want me to put them back?"

Zane nods. "Yeah. I appreciate it."

I give the dogs a few more cuddles as Seth is unleashing them.

"I don't know how you can resist these guys," I tease while jogging back to Zane. "They're so adorable. I'd be in there all day."

He offers me a small smile, and it pierces right through to my heart. Gosh, this man's smile is more powerful than the mountain sun. "I used to. Hell, still do." His smile widens.

I cast him a playful smirk. "I knew it. I'd probably have them in my house, running around all day. They'd destroy everything. But who needs furniture when you have those adorable faces around?"

He laughs out loud, and the sound booms around the yard, echoing between the buildings. "They would go *crazy* inside. Siberian huskies like to be outdoors, and they like the cold. If you coop them up, they'll be miserable. That's why they live out here," he says, pointing to the barn with direct access to the yard.

"Poor things. They would hate it in Florida."

He arches a bushy eyebrow. "You're from Florida?"

"Yup. Fort Lauderdale."

"Oh yeah, no. Way too hot for these mountain guys."

An awkward silence fills the open air. "Well, I'd better get going then. See you tomorrow, I guess?"

"For the lesson?" he asks with a frown.

"Yeah..."

He rubs the back of his neck. "I wasn't sure you'd still want to do that. I'm not exactly a great teacher."

"Your method needs work, yes. But lucky for you, I'm an excellent student." I smile brightly. "I have a week left, and I intend to be the best I can be before I return to my tropical state."

He scratches his head. "We'll see what we can do. Just get some rest tonight, okay? No more training on your own. Exhausting yourself won't do you any good. You need your strength and energy for skiing."

"Got it," I say with a nod. "Don't worry. I'm not putting my skis or my boots back on tonight. Actually, I'm going to a wine tasting." My smile falters. "Which would sound fun if it wasn't for having to explain to yet another person why I'm on my honeymoon alone and not with my husband." Tears brim at the corners of my eyes without warning. I really didn't see them coming. Looks like I can go from peaceful to miserable within the course of a few words. Must be a new skill I developed.

"Please don't cry," Zane says, taking a step toward me. His eyes are swimming with concern and empathy, which immediately makes me cry. I'm so pathetic that even a guy like Zane who clearly lacks social skills can feel sympathy for the pathetic girl who got dumped at the altar. Before I know it, I'm sobbing like a banshee, trying to hide my puffy eyes with my hands.

"I like wine," he says, and that stops the sobbing almost instantly. I feel like a child who's pretend-crying, only I have zero control over my emotions right now.

I dry the tears from my face. "What? You want to come?" I ask, then instantly regret it. That wasn't an offer. There's no way Za—

"Sure." He shoves his hands in his pockets.

I furrow my eyebrows hard, almost closing my eyes in the process. "Really?"

"Unless you don't want me to—"

"No. Yes, I want you," I blurt out louder than I intended.

A small, lopsided grin forms on his lips.

My body heats up, and his intoxicating scent is making me dizzy. Swallowing hard, I add, "To come with me."

He nods. "Okay. Then I will. What time?"

"The tasting starts at seven-thirty," I say, swaying on my feet. "There's also food, I think."

"Okay. I'll be out front of your hotel at seven-twenty, then."

I swallow again, looking down at my boots. "Um, okay. Great. Thank you."

"See you then."

"Bye," I say with a wave before spinning on my heels.

Gosh, that must have been the most awkward exchange in history. And suddenly, I'm burning hot. Even if it's slightly embarrassing that he has to go out of his way to join me so I don't look pathetic, I'm glad and even *looking forward* to tonight. If there's one thing I learned this afternoon, other than a wealth of information about mushing, it's that Zane Harden is full of surprises, and there is actually a nice guy buried underneath all those layers of grouchiness.

Looks like he *is* a good teacher after all.

10

Not That Bad

Zane

I'm not exactly sure why I agreed to attend a wine tasting with Ivy. All I know is I couldn't bear to see her cry. Taking her on a sled ride this afternoon was... well, *nice*. I'd gotten so used to riding by myself, I forgot how gratifying it can be to share the experience with someone who's new to it. I know first-hand how cathartic it can be. Sledding heals all wounds, especially emotional ones. Why do you think I love it so much?

I spot Belinda and Daisy coming back from the grocery store, so I run to give them a hand. Belinda flashes her signature warm smile when she sees me approaching. "My boy, there you are."

"Hey. Sorry, I got held up," I say, picking the bags from her hands.

"Right," Daisy says while rolling her eyes.

I throw her a dark look before following Belinda into the house. "I was on a ride."

"I know. How wonderful," Belinda says. "It's been a while."

I shoot another look at my sister—an annoyed one this time. Of course she told on me. "Why can't you mind your own business?"

"My family *is* my own business," Daisy fires back as we drop the bags on Belinda's kitchen table.

"Not when you're only here a week out of the year," I say through gritted teeth.

"Settle down, you two," Belinda snaps with a stern look, the one a mother would give her children when they're fighting. Which is fitting, considering she pretty much raised us.

Breathing out a long sigh, I start putting away the groceries.

"I don't need Daisy to tell me anything," she says, propping a hand on her hip. "I live across the street. I see it's Seth and not you on that sled every day. I may be old, but I'm not blind."

"Fine," I mutter.

"Besides, you've been spending most of your time here. And I don't think you can split yourself in two yet." She casts me a warm, motherly look. "But I'm glad you're back out there. That's where you belong."

She's not wrong.

"So, why did you go?" Daisy asks, an annoying smirk plastered on her face.

"Do I need to write it in big letters on my forehead or something? *None of your business.*"

"It's that girl, isn't it?" she presses, her eyes gleaming.

Belinda's head snaps toward me like a hawk. She's been on my case about finding a girlfriend for months, so of course when Daisy mentions a girl, she's already getting giddy. "What girl?"

"No one."

"Ha!" Daisy says. "I knew it. If it was really 'no one,' you would have just shrugged and said she's a client."

I brush my hair out of my face. "She *is* a client."

She narrows her eyes. "But you're not shrugging . . ."

I lean back against the counter. Crap. *Why* am I not shrugging? In lieu of an answer, I underline the imaginary sentence written on my forehead.

"Tell me more about this girl," Belinda gushes, sitting down at the table and patting the seat next to her. Then, Daisy mimics her.

"Nope." Placing a kiss on Belinda's head, I get out of there as fast as possible.

It feels weird visiting the touristic part of town at night. I barely go during the day as it is, but I never go at night. As I wait in front of Ivy's hotel, I feel like a teenager waiting for his first date. At least, that's what I assume he'd look like. I didn't really have the typical teenage experience. But I'm pretty sure sweaty palms, dry mouth, and a racing heart would make the cut. Truth is, I'm a little nervous to go wine tasting. I've never done it before. I'll probably look like a fool. Though I did make an effort on my appearance for once. I tied my bushy hair into a man bun, I'm wearing jeans instead of my ski pants, and I swapped my fleece sweater for a flannel shirt—the only one I own. I threw on a black jacket with a fleece interior because, even if I rarely feel the cold, it's particularly chilly tonight.

"Hey," Ivy says from behind me.

I turn around, and my skin prickles as I lay eyes on her. She looks breathtaking. She curled her hair at the bottom, making the copper highlights even more vibrant, and she has some makeup on. Even if I think she's just as beautiful without it, I'm flattered that she did all that for a night out with me.

"Hey," I say with a smile. "Ready?"

She adjusts her pink scarf around her neck. "Yup."

We start our stroll toward the bar, and I take in the strings of beautiful lights twinkling around us. I'm not big on Christmas decorations, but I have to admit, it does look pretty cool. The street is filled with tourists walking to dinner or coming from it, and the atmosphere is relaxed and serene. Far from the Christmas madness I'd been expecting at this hour.

A couple of minutes later, we step into the bar.

"Hi," a young blonde greets with a warm smile. "Do you have a reservation?"

Ivy tenses next to me. "Yes. It's under Ross."

The hostess checks her tablet. "Right. Here it is. Ivy and Dan Ross for wine tasting with a food pairing. And congratulations. Pl—"

"Oh no. He's not the husband. This is Zane," Ivy says, red flaring to her cheeks. "But I'm Ivy, the bride. Well, not really." Her eyes start to water.

"We're friends," I say to the hostess, who gives me a slight nod.

"All right. Please follow me."

Ivy throws me an apologetic look, and I give her a nod, letting her go first. With every step I take in the cramped bar, I feel more and more like a bull in a china shop. Who knew such a place existed in Winter Heights? A sprawling marble bar with a set of green velvet stools occupies the middle of the room, taking up most of the space. The wood paneled walls bear framed paintings of the mountains, and gold-brushed ceiling lamps cast a dim light over the space. A couple of clients look me up and down, but I couldn't care less what they think. I just hope Ivy doesn't feel embarrassed to have me here with her. After all, I did kind of impose my presence.

We're seated in an alcove table, and while I appreciate not being on full display at the bar, the candlelight and "congratulations" card on the table are a bit much. How romantic.

"Good evening," says a tall guy wearing a gray suit. "I'm John, and I'll be your server today. You've booked the deluxe wine-tasting experience, which comes with a sampling of eight of our best bottles as well as some food pairings. I'll bring the first glass over along with some water."

Eight glasses? Geez, are we supposed to slide back home after this?

We thank him politely, and a silence falls between us.

"So, thanks for coming with me," Ivy says, lacing her hands in front of her. "You must think I'm such a loser." She lifts her eyes to me, and my heart softens. I can't imagine the pain she's in right now. Suddenly, I want to break this Dan guy's face in two.

I stare back at her, my gaze latched onto her beautiful eyes. "You're not a loser."

"Of course I am," she says with a lopsided smile. "It's normal to pity someone like me. *I* pity me. Why else would you be here with me tonight? I have a feeling this isn't your typical scene."

I wince. "What gave it away?"

She laughs, and the sound starts to mend the broken pieces inside me.

"I'm here for the booze, by the way. Didn't you hear the guy? Eight glasses of their best wines. Who would say no to that?" I joke, leaning back in my chair. Yeah, like I care about the wine, or know anything about it.

Right on cue, our server comes back with our glasses. The first wine is a Chardonnay. He gives us information about it, but it's beyond my vocabulary. Or my interest, to be honest. When it comes to wine, I'm a simple guy. Either I like it, or I don't.

"Cheers," Ivy says, holding up her drink, and I clink my glass with hers.

"Cheers."

I take a sip of the crisp wine and pick out a few of the nuts the server brought along.

"Thanks again for this afternoon. I had a great time," she says, her expression softening.

"You have to stop thanking me for everything," I tease, suddenly feeling uneasy.

She glances away, biting her lip. "Right. So, your sister seems nice. Does she work with you?"

"Oh no. She's an architect in Chicago and a total nerd. She stayed in school forever. I don't even know how many degrees she has now. She's just here on vacation, but she helps out a little. I only have one employee—Seth, the young guy you met."

She takes a sip of her Chardonnay. "And your brother is a ski instructor?"

"Yes. He got the teaching genes," I say, chuckling.

She narrows her eyes at me, then laughs, and the sound sends tingles through my body. I wish she'd do that more often. "Oh, come on. You're not that bad."

"What about you? Any siblings?"

She nods, grabbing a handful of nuts. "I have a sister, Hazel. She used to be a food critic, but now she's a sous-chef."

I take another long sip of my wine. "Fancy. She lives in Florida too?"

"No. Actually, she lives in France now."

"*Very* fancy. I bet she knows all about wine."

"Yup. Champagne is more her jam, though. But gastronomy has always been part of our lives. Our mom was a foodie, and she made it her mission to pass it on to us. I love food and good restaurants, but it's more Hazel's thing than mine."

"Wow, okay. Full disclosure, I know as much about food as I know about wine."

She chuckles. "I'll teach you what I know."

Her offer makes me smile. Now that I'm starting to get to know her, I realize she's pretty easygoing despite her undoubtedly fancier education compared to mine.

"Have you ever been to France?" she asks, twirling a strand of copper hair around her finger.

"Nope. Never even left the state," I say, rapping my knuckles on the table. "I'm fine right here, in the cold."

She laughs again, the sound bringing a warmth to my chest. "You're pretty much a Siberian husky yourself, aren't you?"

She's not entirely wrong. I don't have a chance to answer because the waiter is now switching our glasses of Chardonnay for Pinot Grigio.

"Maybe I am, but this place is all I know . . ."

"Yeah, I get that. I'll have to go apartment hunting when I get back, and I'm not looking forward to it. Changing your habitat isn't fun," she says, drinking more wine, and I do the same.

I can sense her mood has shifted again. I'm guessing her upcoming move has to do with the deserting husband, so I don't ask. "What do you do for a living? I've ruled out water-skiing instructor, but other than that, the coast is pretty clear."

"Haha. Very funny. I'm a nurse."

I cock my head to the side, studying her. "I can see that."

Her eyes meet mine. "How so?"

"You're nice to people, always in a good mood, and you have empathy." I'm sure she's an excellent nurse. Her patients are lucky to have her. A single smile from Ivy is probably enough to get them back on their feet.

"Well, so do you. You just hide it well."

I bark out a loud laugh, and the old lady sitting next to us shoots me a look of disapproval. I can't help it. No one has ever, in my twenty-eight years of life, called me "nice" or said I had empathy. But I don't disagree. I'm not the warmest guy on the planet, but I *am* nice, and I do have empathy.

"Well, except maybe for the 'good mood' part," Ivy adds with a wink.

With another chuckle, I finish my drink. "You're right about that."

Ivy

"So, how did you get into dog sledding?" I ask when the waiter hustles to our table with our third glass of wine along with a cheese and cold-cut board and warm bread. "That's an unusual job."

"I grew up with it, I guess? The former owner of the farm, Bruce, was my neighbor—he passed away a few years ago—and he took me under his wing. Actually, both Bruce and Belinda helped us out a lot when we were young," he says, taking a slice of cheese.

"Oh, Belinda. The lady who lives across the street?"

He nods. "Yes. They were kind of like substitute parents for us. Our mom was sick all her life, and she died when Daisy was two years old. My dad wasn't really around much."

I'm surprised he's sharing something so personal, and he must feel the same, because he sits up straighter, waving a hand in dismissal. "Anyway, we spent a lot of time with them. I was close with Bruce, so he made sure I behaved. I was the rough one of the lot."

"Really?" I arch an eyebrow. "I would have never guessed that."

"Haha." He casts me a playful glare. "Yeah. So, Bruce let me play with the dogs whenever I skipped school."

"Oh, Bruce was *cool*."

"Very." He laughs, and it feels like the first time I hear his real laugh. It's low and husky, but also warm and sexy. *Stop, Ivy. It's just a laugh.* "Bruce believed in real-world education instead of schoolwork, which worked great for me. He taught me how to mush, which is a lot harder than it looks, but I preferred being out in the snow, taking care of the dogs—even if it was just cleaning their kennels—instead of being cooped up in a room all day. I still do."

"You're not at all like your sister, then."

He smiles, shaking his head. "Nope. Darwin and I used to joke about how we couldn't possibly be related given how studious she was, but that got her pretty upset, so we stopped. With our past, anything's possible, so . . ."

"Well, she has the same eyes as you, and she seems tough, so I'd say she's a Harden all right."

His eyes light up. "That's what we always tell her."

"So, you're pretty close with your siblings too? I know losing our mom and not having a dad made Hazel and me inseparable."

"I'm sorry about your mom," he says before taking a sip of wine. "And your dad."

"Thanks," I say, averting my eyes for a second. The last thing I need is to start crying in front of him. *Again*. "I'm sorry too."

He scratches his beard. "To answer your question, I guess we're pretty close. I see Darwin every day. With Daisy, it's a little different, since she doesn't live here—and because she's a pain in my neck."

I shake my head. "Ah, sisters. That's what they're for. Especially younger ones."

He squints at me. "I take it you're the youngest."

My hand flies to my chest. "I'm offended. Why would you assume that?"

"Because if you were the oldest, you wouldn't say that," he jokes.

I laugh a little too hard, but it's probably the wine. "You're right. I'm the youngest."

He shakes his head. "Knew it." Then, he barks out his sexy laugh again.

Yeah, I've reached a verdict. Zane Harden is not that bad after all.

11

Evolution

Ivy

The next day, I wake up with a skull-splitting headache, but I can easily say that was one of the most fun nights of my life. Zane, after a few drinks, becomes really entertaining and laid-back. He even told me a joke. *A joke.* It was a bad joke, but still. It was something I would have never imagined coming out of his mouth.

I'm downing the rest of my morning coffee in the hotel's breakfast room when I get a text from Hazel.

> **Hazel**
>
> So, how is it going?

> **Ivy**
>
> Good. I had fun yesterday. I went dog sledding, and it was amazing. What about you?

> **Hazel**
>
> We're in Orlando right now, which is always fun. Even if it's packed with tourists. What about that hot ski instructor?

I roll my eyes. I knew she was going to bring that up. Zane claims younger sisters are annoying. Well, older ones are nosy.

> **Ivy**
>
> I never said he was hot. He's actually the owner of the dog sledding farm as well, and we went wine tasting yesterday. It was fun. He's not as grumpy after a few drinks.

> **Hazel**
>
> Ohhhh! Good for you. This vacation sounds like something straight out of a Hallmark movie. But we still

> haven't established whether he's hot or not.

Ivy
> And I'm still not answering.

Hazel
> You just did, sis. Bye.

Grr. She's infuriating. But no matter how much she begs, I'm not admitting Zane's hotness to her. I know Hazel. If I say how sexy he is, she'll pester me about going out with him, rebounding and all that. And I don't want to hear it. I'm not ready, especially not with Zane. That guy's not rebound material. He's crush-your-heart-and-stomp-on-it-with-ski-boots material.

After breakfast, I trudge up to my room, put my equipment on, and meet Zane in front of the hotel.

"Hey," he says, his lips twitching at the corners when he sees me. "Sleep well?"

How can he look this good after the sheer quantity of wine we had last night? "Fine."

His eyes light up. "Oh, someone had a rough night."

I give him a pointed look.

"Well, you'd better be ready," he says, clasping his hands, though the sound is muffled since he's wearing gloves. "We're hitting an actual slope today."

I gasp, covering my mouth with my hand.

"Not a hard one," he adds, probably noticing the panic in my eyes. "But a *real* one."

"Are you sure I'm ready? I'm—"

"You are."

The look in his eyes is so intense, it instantly boosts my confidence.

When we reach the mountain, he takes me on a green run, and I manage to slide down carefully while doing the snowplow, falling only twice. And it's a long run. We do it two more times, and on our last round, I don't even fall once.

"You're doing great." He nods in approval. "I think we can try a new slope."

My eyes widen.

"Still a green but higher on the mountainside. Come on, let's go to the chairlift."

We ski downhill, and I'm still doing great until a kid cuts me off at full speed, throwing me off balance. I roll down the slope, the kid falling with me.

We're a jumbled ball of skis and poles, and it takes me a second to recover.

"Sorry," he says as we both sit down and brush off snow from our frozen faces. He must be around ten years old, from the looks of it. Well, there's no bone-splitting pain in my body, and the kid looks fine. He's already trying to get back on his feet. More fear than harm.

Zane, who was skiing ahead of me, hikes back up, a mean stare simmering in his eyes directed at the kid.

"What were you thinking?" he roars, his deep voice booming around us. "You don't cut people off like that."

The kid seems to shrink into himself. "I—sorry."

"Why are you here alone, anyway?" Zane demands, eyes still blazing with anger.

"I'm not. I'm . . . I'm with my group." He points down the hill to a group of kids clustered around an instructor near the ski lift. The instructor, who's wearing a red-and-white ski suit, waves his poles to us.

"You're with Eric?" Zane turns back to the kid, an eyebrow arched.

He nods fervently.

Zane lets out a low growl. "I'm sure he taught you better than that. Don't do that ever again, or I'll banish you from this mountain, got it?"

Nodding a few more times, the kid clips his ski back on—well, Zane helps him since he's trembling like a leaf—then skis down to his group.

"Are you okay?" Zane asks, his gaze softening the moment it falls on me.

"I'm fine," I say with a chuckle. "So, it's children that you eat for breakfast, huh?"

He stares at me for a second, then rips out a laugh. "Yup. You got me."

After he helps me stand up and put my skis back on, we slide down to the chairlift. I'm happy to report that this lift is a lot easier to board than the drag lift. All you have to do is sit down when they shout at you to. Easy.

It's a bit scarier, though, since you're basically sitting on a bench suspended thirty or forty feet above the ground, your legs dangling. But it's also a lot more spectacular given the stunning views.

"Can you even banish someone from the mountain?" I ask through a giggle, turning to Zane. Maybe he's some sort of royalty here that I don't know about.

He fights a smile. "Of course not."

"Phew. I was starting to get anxious," I say, shoving him in the side.

He scratches his beard. "I was that scary, huh?"

"A little bit," I say with a laugh.

"Well, it was necessary," he says, nodding. "That kid was a public hazard."

I laugh again, warmth spreading through me when I remember the way he protected me. In a shy voice, I ask, "Do you have plans this afternoon?"

"Why?"

"I have a snowmobile excursion booked at two, and then some snow tubing. It could be fun, if you want to come."

He throws me a curious glance. "I don't do tubing, sorry. Way too touristy."

Flames of humiliation heat my cheeks. Right. Just because we went out together once doesn't mean he wants to spend more time with me. My head is so messed up right now. Frankly, I don't even *want* to go snowmobiling. It was Dan's thing. I just thought that maybe, if Zane came . . . Never mind. "No worries. Just thought I'd ask."

He rubs his jaw. "I like snowmobiles, though."

I fight back a smile. "Sorry, you have to agree to the whole touristy package," I tease, even though I'd honestly be happy to hang out with Zane either way.

He smirks, shaking his head. "You drive a tough bargain, Ivy. But I have to draw the line somewhere. If I were you, I'd reconsider, though. Might be a good idea to have a man tagging along. Snowmobiling isn't for the faint of heart."

"What makes you think I don't own a motorcycle at home?" I ask, struggling not to strangle myself with a laugh that threatens to bubble up. The idea of me on a motorcycle is equal parts scary and ridiculous.

He laughs harder, and my stomach does a backflip. Who knew it was that skilled in acrobatics?

Zane's bellowing laughter shakes the bench, and we're suddenly wobbling a little too much for my taste.

"Uh-oh," I say, instinctively gripping his arm.

His laugh dissolves, replaced by the frown he often sports. "You're okay. We're not going to fall," he says, placing an arm around my shoulders. I freeze, unable to react or move an inch. It feels weird, but also nice to have his strong arm around me. I immediately feel safe, and my heartbeat slows. Letting out a long sigh, I say, "Thank you. That was kind of terrifying."

I expect him to withdraw his arm, but he keeps it firmly in place, and I'm not about to complain. Being held by Zane is something else.

"So, have I made my case?" he asks, giving me a pointed look.

I roll my eyes, biting my lip to contain my smile. "Shut up."

He chuckles, staring ahead to admire the view, and I do the same while simultaneously attempting to chase the butterflies out of my belly.

"I'm curious now," he says as we're approaching the top of the lift. "Do you own a motorcycle?"

I chuckle, shaking my head. "No, but that's beside the point. Women are just as capable as men at handling heavy machinery." Not that I'm personally interested, but still.

He nods. "I won't argue with that. Belinda had one, and she would take us out on trips every weekend. It's not as fun as sledding with the dogs, but it's a close second. If you've never driven a motorcycle before, though, it can be a little scary, that's all."

Wow. Belinda sounds like a rockstar. "Fine, you can skip the tubing and come for the snowmobiling." I cave, partly because I'll take as much Zane time as I can, and partly because I wasn't that into the idea of snowmobiling in the first place, and his comments only made it worse.

Zane

I had to stand my ground on tubing. What could be more touristy than barreling down the hill on an inner tube, giggling and screaming? I'm a local, a mountain man. That's beneath me. I can't be reduced to that level, but I almost caved and said yes. Ivy looked so hopeful and gorgeous. I have a feeling that refusing her anything is a major struggle. Or maybe it's just me.

"My boy," Belinda says, opening her front door. I told her I would stop by for lunch. "How are you, my boy?" She gives me a long hug, and I kiss her on the cheek.

"I'm good. Just finished a lesson. And you?"

"Fine, fine. Went down to Mrs. Carr's to play cards this morning. We had fun."

"Did you win?" I already know the answer. Belinda is a fierce sore loser, so if she says she had fun, it can only mean one thing.

"Of course I did," she says with a laugh.

I follow her down to the kitchen, where the smell of smoked sausage one-pot casserole fills the room.

"Smells good in here."

"Thank you," she says, opening the lid to stir the pot's contents. "It'll be ready in a few minutes if you want to go outside to see Boomer."

She doesn't have to tell me twice. I've known Boomer ever since I first started mushing. He was just a puppy at the time.

I slide the door to the back porch open, and Boomer stands up from his favorite corner when he sees me. He slowly hobbles toward me. Far gone are the times when he would scamper and jump all over me, and my heart constricts at the reminder.

"Hey, bud," I say, scratching his face and petting him. He lies down and rolls onto his back. "Yeah. You like that, huh? You're so handsome, aren't you?"

He barks in response and gets up to lick my cheek.

I stay out there for a while, giving him some love and talking to him until Belinda calls out that lunch is ready.

We sit down to eat, and as always, the food is delicious. Belinda is an excellent cook. She tried to show me a trick or two, but I don't have the patience for it.

"So, are you going on a ride this afternoon?" she asks.

I take a bite of moist, smoky sausage. "No. I'm going snowmobiling with a friend, actually."

She shoots me a smirk. "A friend, huh?"

Here we go. I knew this was coming, but frankly, it's better if I rip off the Band-Aid now. As long as Daisy isn't here to add her grain of salt into it. I can't seem to have friends when it comes to her.

"Yes." I return her pointed look. "A friend."

She arches an eyebrow. "Is she the same friend you took on a ride yesterday?"

"Yup," I say, now purposefully avoiding her gaze.

"I thought you said she was a client," Belinda says with an innocent tone.

"Well, that evolved into friendship, I guess. Or acquaintanceship? If that's a thing."

I can tell she's trying to conceal her smile, which makes my pulse pound harder. Why is everyone so interested in my friendship—or acquaintanceship—with Ivy?

"I see. What's her name?"

"Ivy," I mutter, her name burning my lips. "She's on vacation here from Florida."

She frowns, putting her fork down to grab her glass. "Alone?"

"Yeah. From what I understand, it was supposed to be her honeymoon? But her fiancé bailed last minute."

Belinda winces. "Poor girl." With a softer voice, she adds, "Be careful, though. Someone who's just passing through and who just got out of a complicated relationship isn't someone you want to get involved with."

I almost choke on a sausage. Tapping on my chest, I cough and wash it down with some water. "I'm not getting involved with anyone."

"I'm just looking out for you, my boy." She places her hand over mine. "Don't want to see you hurt again."

"I know," I say, putting my other hand on top of hers. She's always looked out for me, and I'm so lucky to have her in my life. "You have nothing to worry about. I'm just keeping Ivy company because she's alone, that's all."

Which is perfectly true. There's nothing else going on. She's my client—and my friend, I guess—but the evolution stops there. I remember all too well how a broken heart feels, and I'm not about to let that happen again.

12

Enjoy The Ride

Ivy

After lunch, I meet Zane at the snowmobile company's storefront, which sits at the very end of the main street. I'd be lying if I said I wasn't nervous. What was I thinking, inviting him? We had fun at the wine tasting, but that was a one-time deal. He has a life. I can't expect him to join me for every activity I have planned for my vacation. Yet here he is, looking glorious as ever, even if this is the first time I've seen him wrapped in so many layers. He seems to have doubled in size beneath his thick coat, gloves, and a beanie.

"That's a lot of clothes," I joke as he strides up to me.

"Snowmobiling is even colder than sledding," he says, looking me up and down. "Are you sure you won't get cold in that?"

Not if you keep looking at me like that, I won't. Of course, I don't say that out loud. Instead, I chirp, "Yep. I have thermal clothing underneath."

His eyes darken, but he doesn't say anything more.

"Let's go, I guess," I say with a shrug.

He frowns. "You don't sound very enthusiastic."

I try to smile, but it comes out as a grimace. "That's my 'scared-to-death' tone."

"Why would you book a snowmobile ride if you're scared?"

"It's . . . Um, I didn't choose this one." Why does Dan always sneak back into my thoughts? Haven't I suffered enough?

A short silence falls between us.

"Right. Good thing I'm here, then." He winks, and I roll my eyes. "I knew you'd need me. Don't worry. We'll have fun."

He pushes the shop door open, and I follow him inside.

A man with black hair and deep blue eyes pops up from under the counter. There must be something in the water here, or maybe it's my hormones, but Winter Heights men are incredibly attractive. "Zane! What are you doing here?"

"Hey, Ethan," Zane says, walking toward him and shaking his hand. "Just here with a friend." He glances at me, and my insides burn. Friend? He views me as his friend? I guess we *are* kind of friends now. The sound of my name pulls me out of my thoughts.

"Hi," I say, shaking Ethan's hand. "Nice to meet you."

"Likewise." Ethan glances between Zane and me curiously. "So, you want to ride?"

"Yes," Zane says. "Ivy has a booking, actually."

Ethan's eyes light up. "Oh, yes. My two o'clock. I didn't know it was with you. Well, this changes things. If you guys want to go on your own, you can."

"On—on our own?" I sputter, trying to hide the terror in my voice. Snowmobiling is the one thing I dreaded on this trip. I don't like motor engines, especially loud, fast ones. But Dan was so enthusiastic at the idea that I reluctantly agreed. It was a trip for both of us, after all. Or so I thought.

"I usually come along," Ethan says. "I take you on a trail, and you follow me. But Zane here knows the mountain as well as I do, maybe better, so you don't need a guide."

"We'll be fine," Zane says, slapping Ethan's back. "But maybe we should just take one snowmobile?" He glances at me.

I nod, relieved. "One. Yes, I think it's better if I'm not driving."

"Are you sure?" Ethan asks. "I can easily give you two. You only need a driver's license, which I already have on file, and you booked for two."

"I'm positive. You can keep the money for the second one, it's fine. I'm more comfortable as a passenger." After coming to Winter Heights, I decided to do the activity just to prove to myself I could, and that I didn't need a man. But in this instance, I'm glad I have one.

"All right. I'll go get it ready for you. Zane, can you find helmets for the both of you?"

Zane nods, ambling over to the helmet wall on the side of the shop and surveying the sizes.

Once Ethan steps outside to get the snowmobile ready, I walk up to Zane. "So, you and Ethan are friends, huh?"

"We go way back. He was born in this town, just like me. He's one of my brother's best friends. Here," Zane says, tucking a helmet on my head.

"Thanks."

He grabs a second one for himself, and we meet Ethan outside. The snowmobile is bigger than I imagined, and somehow that makes it a little less scary. At least it should be stable.

"I don't need to tell you the rules," Ethan says to Zane. "Just be careful, okay?"

"Of course," Zane says, hopping on the engine.

Ethan retreats into the shop, and I stay frozen, looking at the snowmobile and the spot right behind Zane where I'm supposed to sit. Suddenly, this snowmobile doesn't scare me nearly as much as the butterflies swarming in my belly. I'm going to be holding on to Zane, wrapping my arms around his waist.

Zane pats the spot behind him. "Hop on. It'll be fine. I won't go fast, I promise."

I swallow hard. That's not what I'm worried about. I straddle the snowmobile a few inches away from him, only placing my hands on his waist.

He turns around and shoots me a curious look. "Are you going to tickle me, or are we going for a ride?"

I shake my head. "What?"

"You can't go snowmobiling with a weak grip like that. If you don't hold on, you will fall, and you'll most likely die."

My eyes widen, and he laughs. "Come on. Hold on tight." He grabs my hands and snakes them around his waist, forcing my body to connect with his. Sure, we're both wrapped in thick layers of clothing, but it still feels incredibly intimate. Or maybe it's just my messed-up brain talking.

After all, Zane looks perfectly relaxed. There is no flirtiness in his attitude. I'm the only one who's getting all worked up.

He puts his goggles on. "Ready?"

"Just be careful, okay?" I plead, doing the same.

"Don't worry." He pats my hand gripping his stomach. "It'll be fun. Hold on; we're going now."

"But you didn't—"

The snowmobile departs, making zero sound. "Wait. It's an electric engine?"

"Yeah," Zane says. "The only ones allowed in our town. We have to preserve all this beautiful nature."

The fact that there's no motor roaring and vibrating beneath me makes the experience a lot less scary, and I love that they're enforcing these kinds of changes to protect the environment. I didn't even know this was a thing.

Zane was right—snowmobiling is fun. After riding a few miles in a half frightened-to-death, half awestruck state, I'm finally able to relax and enjoy the scenery. We reach a trail, and suddenly, I'm back in my enchanted forest from the sledding trip yesterday. How cool is it to have the chance to experience this? The snow-capped trees whiz by us, and as they become a blur with the speed of the engine, a freeing sensation overpowers me.

The snow is untouched for miles, and right now, it feels like we're the only ones in the entire world. The only sound hitting our ears is the rustling of dead leaves clinging to the bare branches and the swoosh of the snow below us. Zane speeds up, but I don't mind. It's exhilarating. He was right, it does get chillier on the snowmobile. But with Zane acting as my own personal heater, I barely notice the cold. I tighten my grip around his waist and press my cheek to his back, enjoying the ride.

13

Brave

Zane

Ivy relaxes with each passing mile, and I soon get used to her arms around my waist. I tried to hide the effect her proximity had on me so she wouldn't feel nervous riding with me, but that was easier said than done. It's been a while since I've been this close to anyone, and I didn't think I missed it until now. But the way Ivy holds on behind me, completely relaxed, fills a hollow pit I didn't know I had. And it's the perfect fit.

Unfortunately, our time with the snowmobile is almost up. Spotting a family of deer peering through the nearby aspen trees, I stop the vehicle and point to them.

"Oh," Ivy whispers. "They're so cute."

They really are. That's one of the reasons why I love riding the mountain trails. Few tourists come up here, and you really get to come face to face with nature. There's nothing more beautiful than that. Except maybe the slight flush on Ivy's face right now as she watches Mama Deer licking her fawn. Ivy's eyes are sparkling so brilliantly, they ignite something inside me. I love how much she appreciates nature even though she lives in a city. I saw it during the sled ride, and I'm witnessing it again now. Not that I'd understand how you couldn't be in awe of such beauty. Still, it's something I would have never thought we had in common when we first met.

They cross in front of us, casting us curious glances. We don't move a muscle, not wanting to scare them off. The little fawn isn't too reassured, though, and tries speeding up across the trail, but his tiny legs wobble, and he stumbles a couple of times. Finally reaching the other side, they disappear into the thick of the forest.

"That was so cool," Ivy breathes, looking at me.

I nod, then check my watch. "Sorry to say, but we're going to have to head back. We've already extended our time a little."

"Oh, yeah. Let's go," she says, hugging me again.

"How about you drive us back?"

Her hands freeze, and I feel her body go rigid. "What? No. I'm good right here."

I'm good too, but I want her to have the experience of driving it herself. I know she's not too confident, but she can handle it. If anything, Ivy has shown me that she's a tough cookie. The very fact that she's here alone after her idiot ex-fiancé left her is testament to that.

"Come on," I say, angling myself to glance at her. "It's fun. You'll be great, and you don't have to go fast."

She draws her bottom lip between her teeth. "Are you sure?"

I hop off the snowmobile. "Absolutely."

Her mouth twists to the side as she's clearly pondering the possibility in her head, until she finally nods and slides forward on the seat.

That's my girl.

I show her the controls, then settle in behind her. Now it's my turn to hold on to her, which feels a lot more intimate than the other way around. "Um. Is this okay? I'm not holding too tight?" I ask, clearing my throat.

"No." Her voice is slightly more high-pitched than usual. I guess she's still a little scared after all.

"Okay, let's go. Don't worry."

With a nod, she puts her goggles on, presses on the accelerator, and off we go. She's hesitant at first, or maybe just cautious, but then she speeds up, and I can feel her body relax in my arms.

She even yells, "Woo-hoo!" clearly enjoying the ride. Warmth seeps into my chest as she drives us back toward the shop. She wasn't very excited to go at first, but I think she'll have a good memory of this snowmobile trip, which was my entire motive for joining her. She's brave enough to do this on her own, and I want her to love every second of it.

The shop comes into sight, and Ivy parks the snowmobile in front of the store. Her parking skills still need some work—we're blocking the entryway—but that's beside the point.

"That was fun," Ivy gushes, getting down and taking her helmet off. She shakes her wavy hair, sending up whiffs of her shampoo, and the way it mingles with the fresh pine scent of the air is exquisite. I wish I could bottle that scent and spray it around my house. Wait. What is wrong with me? All this human interaction is clearly getting to my head.

Coming to my senses, I take my gear off. "Told you."

Ethan marches out of the shop. "How was it?"

We tell him about our trip, and Ivy's eyes sparkle as she relates our deer encounter.

"Glad you enjoyed the ride," he says. "By the way, here's a refund for the second snowmobile." He hands her some bills.

"Oh no," Ivy says, waving her hands. "There's no need. I booked for two. It's my fault."

"Please," he says, placing the bills in her hand. "I insist. Go for coffee or a snack with this one." He throws me a look. "It's not often we see him hanging around this part of town. He needs to let loose a little."

"Oh, come on," I grumble, rolling my eyes. Why is everyone so determined to interfere with my life? Maybe *that's* why I don't go out much.

Ivy laughs, and my focus instantly returns to her. "Okay. I will. Thank you so much."

"You're welcome. Take care," he says, shooting me a wink before going back inside. I resist the urge to roll my eyes again, but considering the way my heart is racing in my chest, I'd say I'm not one hundred percent angry about Ethan's interference.

"Thanks again for coming with me," Ivy says as we start back toward the town center. "I owe you a coffee." She holds up the money in front of me with a smile. "Should we meet up after my tubing session? Or maybe you have stuff to do? I can take a rain check, or we can just skip it altogether, whatever." With every word that comes out of her mouth, she turns more pink, and my heart beats faster. She shoves her hands in her coat pockets, looking away.

"We can grab a coffee after we go tubing," I mumble, completely baffled by the words that escape my mouth.

She does a double take. "You're coming tubing with me?" she squeals.

"Shhh." I glance around. "Not so loud. I don't want anyone to overhear you." And I'm only half joking about that.

She props a hand on her waist. "People will see you there, you know. You're not exactly easy to conceal."

I chuckle. "Trust me, no one from the village goes snow tubing."

"Then why are you coming?"

"I believe I'm owed a coffee and a snack."

She just laughs. "Right. Okay, then. Let's go. I have a feeling some good old childish fun will do you good."

14

Good Timing

Zane

Who knew snow tubing could be this fun? The tubing hill is full of tourists—mostly kids—but the way Ivy lights up when she slides down the lane is a reward in itself. We're going up again, and she bugs me to ride on a double tube with her because it'll slide faster with two people.

"I thought you hated speed," I say with a grunt.

"I don't *hate* speed. I just don't like when moving vehicles—or rides—go too fast. Tubing is different. Plus, nothing can happen to us."

"Fine."

I sit on the back hoop and she in the front, and down we go. She was right about the speed, but not the part where nothing can happen to us. When we reach the little bump near the middle of the lane, the tube flips, and we land on the packed snow. Or rather, I land on the snow, and she lands right on top of me. Her face is inches from mine, her long brown hair framing her face, and her lips hovering way too close to mine. We lock eyes for a second, then she starts giggling until it turns into full-blown laughter. She rolls off of me and lies on the slope.

"Are you okay?" she asks, sitting up.

"Yeah. You?" *Aside from the fact that I was thinking of kissing you two seconds ago.* The fact that I was *this* close to leaning forward and closing the gap between us scares me to death. I have never been that close to kissing someone—or even thinking about it—since Sofia. My stomach twists, and I chase Sofia from my thoughts.

Ivy nods. "Good. But I think I'm ready for some food now. Should we go?"

Forcing myself to focus, I get up and offer Ivy a hand. "Absolutely."

"The Christmas market? *Really*?" I whine as we approach the park that has now been overtaken by holiday music and cinnamon fumes.

"What do you have against Christmas?" she asks, arching an eyebrow. "Or this market? It looks cute."

It is pretty cool, I guess. I've never been here, even though they've been setting it up every year for a while now. It's just not really my vibe. Quaint chalets of vendors selling local delicacies and handmade products with dozens of kids running around isn't exactly my scene. Though, I could see myself taking Aaron here.

"Let's start with hot chocolate," she says, her eyes going as wide as her smile. We stop by a stand that's making hot drinks in reusable white mugs with trees and other Christmas symbols stamped on them.

An old lady I don't recognize greets us with a warm smile. "What can I get you?"

"Hi," Ivy says. "I'll have a hot cocoa with marshmallows, please."

The woman nods, then looks at me.

"I'll get some coffee. Black."

"Zane," Ivy scolds. "That's not very Christmassy."

"Christmas is over," I say with a shrug.

She gives me a pointed look. "Only if you let it be."

I want to say that she's wrong, that Christmas is a date on the calendar and not a mood, but I don't want to be a downer. "I'm good with coffee. I don't like sweet stuff."

"Of course you don't," she says, rolling her eyes.

Minutes later, we get our drinks and begin our stroll around the market.

Ivy takes a sip of her hot chocolate. "Mmm. Delicious. You have to try it."

"I'm good with my coffee."

"Oh, come on. I went snowmobiling, didn't I? Now it's your turn to trust me." Her smile widens, and she waggles her eyebrows in a goofy way.

Well, I guess I'm drinking hot chocolate.

With a grumble, I grab the mug and bring it to my lips. A warmth fills me, the sweet taste settling on my tongue like a blanket of nostalgia. I haven't had hot cocoa since I was a kid, when Belinda would make it for us after we played outside in the snow for a while. Ivy's right. It's really good. A little too sweet, but comforting.

She stares at me with a questioning look.

"It's all right," I say, giving her the mug back.

"All right?" She looks down at her mug. "You drank almost half of it."

I shrug. "My mouth is just bigger. I'll get you another one."

"No need," she says with a grin. "Plus, Ethan gave me plenty of money. I'm treating you today. You've been so kind to keep me company, both today and yesterday at the wine tasting. This trip has been so embarrassing, you have no idea. I really didn't think this through, coming here alone." She lets out a nervous chuckle, tucking a strand of loose hair behind her ear.

"Can I ask what happened?" I don't want to make her relive it, but I just can't comprehend why anyone would let this girl go when they're about to get married to her.

She sighs, her gaze drifting. "He was in love with someone else."

"But he asked you to marry him?" I grimace. Could this guy be any dumber?

Her face scrunches. "I know. It's weird, right?"

"Yeah . . ." That's an understatement.

"He was still hung up on his ex. She went back to him the night before our wedding, and he called me to let me know."

My blood freezes in my veins. "Wait. He didn't even tell you face to face?"

"Nope," she blurts out in a single breath. "But Dan was never really a frank person so . . ." She clears her throat. "It was just very bad timing."

"Or good timing?" I suggest, raising an eyebrow. "At least you didn't have to get a divorce."

"Yeah, I guess you're right. Who's the one with a positive attitude now?" she jokes, shoving me with her shoulder.

I let out a grunt. "I spend way too much time with you. And you make me drink sweet stuff."

"Then my work here is almost done." She chuckles, and I tense at the thought that she's going home in a few days. Soon, this will just be a memory. "But seriously. Thanks again for everything. I've had a lot of fun these past few days."

"Me too." My stomach twists as I say the words.

"Oh, ice skating!" She points to the side of the park where a large ice skating rink is filled with people. "That looks like fun."

"Absolutely not." I hold a hand up, careful not to spill my coffee. "Don't push it. We already did tubing. That's enough for one day."

"All right," she says. "What about a bite to eat?"

I relax my shoulders. "I never say no to food."

15

Awkward

Zane

After some food and one more lap around the market, I walk Ivy back to her hotel, drawing in a gasp when I see the time on my watch. "How is it already nine p.m.?"

"I know." She chuckles as we stop in front of the hotel. "I just saw that too. Time flies."

"It does."

Our eyes lock, and all I want right now is to find out how sweet her lips would taste. Probably as sweet as that second hot cocoa. My mouth waters at the thought. This is the second time I've thought of kissing her in the last few hours, and I'm really starting to worry about my mental health.

Her gaze roves from my eyes to my lips, then back to my eyes. I lean forward, but she takes a step back. "Thanks for walking me," she says, pressing her lips in a thin line. "I'll see you tomorrow for my lesson."

I rake a hand through my hair. "Right. Of course. Good night."

I cuss at myself all the way home. How stupid am I to make that kind of move? She just broke up with her fiancé, and not by choice. Of course she doesn't want to kiss me. She's just looking for a friend. Heck, *I'm* just looking for a friend.

I don't realize I'm home until Daisy's voice startles me.

"Hey. You're home late. At least by your standards, grandpa."

She's lounging on the couch, watching TV.

"*You're* up late," I counter, sitting at the end of the couch. "Haven't seen you awake past ten since you got here."

She stretches her arms above her head, yawning. "I know. I was just thinking about Todd and everything, and I lost track of time."

I fix my eyes on her. "What happened, Daisy? Why is he not here? Did you guys break up?" I ask, concern taking over. I was never a fan of the guy, but I don't want my sister to suffer, and the thought of her living alone in Chicago makes me uneasy.

"I told you," she says, picking at the fabric of the blanket that's covering her. "He had to work."

I give her a pointed look borrowed from Belinda.

She sighs, jerking the cover off. "Fine. I'm leaving him."

My eyes bulge in their sockets. "What?"

"I didn't want to say anything because my decision wasn't final, but it is now. He's been treating me like crap for a while. I just have to get out of this."

The situation is way worse than I thought. "What did he do?" I growl. In other words, what will I be breaking his face for? "I'll hop on the next flight to Chicago and go kick his ass."

"Calm down." She rolls her eyes, though the corners of her lips pull into a small smile. "That's why I didn't want to tell you. It wouldn't do any good. It'd just add fuel to the fire."

"What fire, Daisy?" I slide down to properly sit on the couch. When she leans her head against my shoulders, I wrap my arm around her. "What's going on? What did he do?"

"It's not just one thing. It's how he is. One day, he makes me feel like the most precious, amazing girl on earth. And the next, I'm this worthless, good-for-nothing country girl." She sighs. "I didn't even notice what was happening for a while, but then it got more and more intense. Lucy told me I was making a mistake moving in with him, and she was right. Now it's just a mess."

"What are you going to do?" I ask, rubbing her arm. "Do you even have a place to live?"

"Well, I'm staying at my big brother's house for the time being," she jokes, poking me in the chest. "But I'm moving in with Lucy when I go back. I'll be fine."

"Or you could stay?"

She sighs again. "What about my job? Plus, I love Chicago. I want to go back."

"Okay. Well, I'm glad you got out of that situation. Let me know if you change your mind on that butt-kicking. I'd be on a plane the next day."

"So, that's what it'd take to get you to come visit me, huh?"

I admit, the idea of hopping on a plane and flying to a huge city is one of the most unappealing things on the planet for me. But for my little sister, of course I would.

"Oh yeah. The prospect of teaching that jerk a lesson is enough fuel for me. Haven't you heard? I'm a teacher now."

She shakes her head. "Don't worry about it. I really just want to put this all behind me."

I nod in understanding, squeezing her arm. "Well, now I get why you brought so much crap with you," I joke.

She chuckles in my arms. "Yeah. To be honest, I thought that'd give me away the second I arrived."

"I'm not too good at reading signals," I say, recalling that I didn't understand why Ivy was alone on her honeymoon. Weirdly, that feels like weeks ago when really, it's only been a few days.

"What about you and Sofia?" she asks.

My body tenses at the mention of her name.

"You don't have to tell me." She places her hand on my forearm softly.

I clear my throat. I wish I could tell her, but the words stay stuck in my throat. "There's not a lot to say. I'm better off alone. You know me."

"Yeah . . . What about that girl?" she asks, cocking her head. "Ivy. What's going on with her?"

My throat constricts, and I look away. "Nothing."

She raises an eyebrow. "If you want to lie to me, Zane, you'll have to do better than that."

"Nothing happened," I say with a shrug. "She's here on vacation. Actually, her honeymoon."

Her eyebrows draw together. "Wait. What?"

"Ivy's fiancé deserted her the night before the wedding, and she decided to come on her own. That's the other reason why nothing could ever happen."

"Whoa. Yeah, I can imagine."

I stare into the fireplace. "I guess she and I are friends."

"Look at us. We're the kind of siblings who talk about their feelings after all," Daisy says with a faint smile.

I chuckle, bumping my shoulder with hers. "Huh. Who knew?"

Ivy

The lump in my throat grows bigger with every step toward the meeting point for my ski lesson. There definitely was a vibe yesterday, and I thought Zane was going to kiss me. Even crazier, I *wanted* him to kiss me. So badly. But at the last second, I chickened out. Kissing Zane—or anyone—is the last thing I should be doing right now. My life is complicated enough as it is.

When I arrive at the base of the slope, however, every ounce of awkwardness in me vanishes. Zane is acting perfectly normal, and we both have a great time during my ski lesson. I learn to do turns using poles. It's a lot harder than I thought, meaning most of the time, I'm rolling down the hill instead of skiing.

"That wasn't too bad," Zane says as we're taking our equipment off.

I shoot him a look of mock indignation. "Are you kidding? I was more down than up today."

He grimaces. "Well, there's definitely room for improvement, but you're doing good. Learning to ski takes time and practice."

"You're well on your way to becoming a very good teacher, you know? Your siblings would be proud."

He shakes his head, chuckling.

"So, are you busy now?" I ask before I can stop myself. I swore that I wouldn't ask him to come to yet another couple's activity, yet here I am, unable to shut up.

"Not really. I mean, I have work, but with Daisy helping out, I have a little more time on my hands."

"Do you like to cook?"

"I like to eat," he says with a chuckle. "I cook a little, I guess. But let me put it this way—I cook like you ski."

That draws a laugh out of me. "You must set the kitchen on fire then. But actually, that's perfect."

He frowns, though his eyes are shining with a suppressed smile. "Really?"

"I have a cooking class in a little bit," I say, wringing my hands. Why am I suddenly so nervous? I've been shameless about asking him to step in for every other activity. What's one more? Plus, it won't be nearly as romantic as our evening out yesterday. "A chef will teach us a few recipes, we'll cook, and then we'll eat what we made."

He quirks an eyebrow. "There's a cooking class in Winter Heights?"

"Sure there is. It's in my hotel's restaurant."

"Well, I'll come along. I'm not saying I'll be much of a cook, but why not? It's never too late to learn something new."

My heart leaps at the thought of spending more time with Zane. He's the only reason this holiday hasn't been a complete disaster, ending every night with me, a bottle of champagne, and a carton of ice cream.

We walk back to my hotel and chat about his cooking skills, which are apparently far from those of my sister's fiancé. I stop by my room to freshen up and change, Zane waiting for me in the lobby. Apparently, he didn't even break a sweat this morning, so he doesn't need to change. Shocker.

There are two other couples in the waiting room when we arrive. Marius and Jo—a recently retired couple from LA—and Jude and Lina, who look to be about our age, from the UK.

"What brings you here today?" Jo asks us with a warm smile. "My husband and I are celebrating our thirtieth wedding anniversary, and we thought it was time we start learning how to cook," she jokes, and we all laugh. "We've been too busy working all our lives and raising our children, so now we're taking some time for ourselves."

"Your cooking is super, honey," her husband says, kissing her temple. "But, yes. Taking our retirement has been the best decision of our lives."

"Well, my fiancé is quite the baker," Lina announces with an American accent, gazing fondly at Jude. "I try my best to keep up with him, but baking is tough. Cooking seems more freestyle, and I think that might be more my jam."

"Always selling yourself short," Jude says, his deep British accent warming the room. Lina just shakes her head and leans against him.

Zane clears his throat, and I look between him and the rest of the group. I guess it's our turn. I stammer, "We, um.

I don't have a lot of cooking experience, though I'm still alive after all my attempts, so that's something." A weird, high-pitched laugh bubbles out of me.

"And I am terrible at cooking. I don't even know what I'm doing here," Zane blurts, making everyone laugh.

"How long have you two been together?" Jo asks, her eyes trailing between Jude and Lina, then Zane and me. "You both make beautiful couples."

"We've been together for three years," Jude says with a smile. "And loving every second of it."

Four pairs of eyes fall on me, and my breathing accelerates. Why can't people mind their own business? And why isn't the chef here so we can cut this conversation short?

I take a small intake of breath, my cheeks burning. "We—I—"

"A couple of years," Zane says, placing an arm around my shoulders. I stare at him, and he just winks. "It's our honeymoon, actually."

"Oh, how wonderful," Jo says.

My erratic breathing evens out, soothed by Zane's arm around me, his fresh mountain scent, and the fact that he just blatantly lied to these people so I wouldn't have to put my pathetic self on display. Again. I throw him a grateful look, and he just squeezes my shoulders, sending a flock of butterflies fluttering in my stomach.

16

Marvelous Giu

Zane

I hope I didn't cross a line just now, lying about us being together, but I hate that Ivy has to suffer through this over and over again. She doesn't deserve the pain that jackass inflicted on her. I want to smash in his stupid face with a snow shovel for hurting her this way.

Jude and Lina are telling us about their wedding planned for next year when a tall, dark-haired guy with a curled mustache enters the small waiting room. He's wearing a chef uniform and a white hat. "*Buongiorno a tutti*. Welcome to the everyday cooking class," he booms in a louder voice than necessary before flashing his pearly whites.

A collective "hello" follows from the women and Marius. The British dude, Jude, just looks at him, and I hold back a groan. This chef looks way too cheerful for my liking.

"I am Chef Giuseppe, but you can call me Giu. First, let's start by calling the roll. Like at school, no?" he chuckles. *"Allora*, I have Hollywood stars Marius and Jo from LA."

Everyone but Jude and me chuckle at his quip. How long is this cooking class again?

"That's us," Jo says with a smile.

"Perfetto. Next, Lina and Jude, the British royals."

Lina raises her hand while Jude rolls his eyes.

"And finally, our honeymoon couple from Florida, Ivy and Dan. Congratulations."

"Actually," I cut in, "it's Ivy and Zane."

"Oh, *dio mio*. Sorry about that; probably a mistake. It happens with the phone bookings because of the spotty connection. Unless the lady changed husbands already," he adds, making everyone laugh.

Ivy forces a smile.

"Right. *Allora*, follow me to the kitchen, and we can make the magic happen."

We all file into a large kitchen with white-tiled walls and long, stainless-steel kitchen counters. Atop the cooking surface are various utensils and ingredients, forming three separate stations.

Giu hands each of us an apron and a hat, which I refuse to put on. I'm not the only one, though. Jude refuses the hat too. I'm starting to like this dude.

We take our positions behind the counters. Ivy and I are next to the Californian couple, and the British pair is across from us.

Giuseppe clasps his hands together. "We are going to make *l'ulitmo piatto* from the Italian cuisine, *la pasta*." He gestures way too widely, and I'm starting to wonder if this is some kind of joke. I mean, who is this guy? I've never seen him around here before.

"Oh, I love pasta," Jo says.

"We will make, more specifically, ravioli from scratch. *Con* ricotta and spinach. First, we need to prepare the dough. Then, we will create the garnish and cook the sauce." He then starts rambling really fast in Italian, and we're all completely lost, though I'm pretty sure he's just talking to himself as he gathers ingredients from the cold storage room.

Ivy glances up, clearly struggling not to break into a laugh. At least it's not just me.

I pinch my fingers together, mimicking the famous Italian hand gesture, and Ivy buries her face in my arm to muffle her laughter. I can't hold back my goofy grin.

Giuseppe strides back out and first instructs Ivy on how to prepare the dough for the pasta. It's actually pretty easy. You only need flour, eggs, and salt. We layer some flour on the counter, then crack a few eggs and a pinch of salt on top before mixing it all together.

And just when I thought I was getting the hang of it, the process quickly becomes more complicated.

"Um." Ivy frowns, looking at me. "Am I doing this right?"

Her hands are full of gooey dough. It doesn't look even close to the finished product, which is a firm, smooth dough. I glance at our neighbors, and they're all in better shape than us. The Brits almost have their dough finished.

"I think we just have to knead it with a little more muscle."

"*Siiii*," Giuseppe exclaims, appearing next to me. "You have to knead harder. Like this."

He places his hands on top of Ivy's, helping her knead the dough with a firmer touch. Blood pulses in my veins, and I suddenly want to slice his hands with that large knife on the counter.

Fortunately, the dough almost instantly starts to take shape. "But you take my place, Husband," he says, probably seeing the flames in my eyes.

Gladly.

He steps aside, and I stand behind Ivy, placing my hands on hers trying not to collide with her body, but it's not an easy task. I barely have time to adjust to her touch and the tormenting smell of her hair when Giuseppe shouts again. "Now, knead. Come on! You have big muscles. Use them."

A low growl escapes me, and Ivy shivers. It's subtle, and if I wasn't this close to her, I wouldn't have even noticed. Probably the effect of Giuseppe's annoying pitch.

We start kneading the dough with more pressure, which is a lot harder than it sounds. I don't have that much of a grip. For one, I'm standing a good three inches behind Ivy so that I don't accidentally hug her from behind and make this situation even more uncomfortable than it already is. Second, I'm literally afraid to break Ivy's delicate fingers in the process. Giuseppe is right. I do have big muscles, but I don't always measure my strength. Roughing around with fifty-pound dogs every day doesn't help.

"Get in there," Giuseppe bellows. Why is he still here? "Make love to the dough," he adds. "And to your woman."

I glance up at him, and he just winks. Is this guy for real? Seriously, where are the hidden cameras?

I close the gap between Ivy and me. "Is this okay?" I whisper in her ear. Goosebumps erupt along her collarbone as she nods.

"Tell me if I'm hurting you," I breathe as I start to knead harder.

"*Si*. There you go. It's working." Giuseppe clasps his hands, watching the dough forming beneath our palms.

We keep at it, and I'm finally getting more comfortable with the situation, enjoying the warmth radiating from her body. Suddenly, images flash through my mind before I can stop them. Ivy and me, cooking at home, her hugging me tight. Ivy sitting on my lap, throwing her head back as she laughs at a stupid joke I made.

"Okay! Done," Giuseppe exclaims, pulling me out of my trance. Could this guy be any more annoying?

I take a wide step back, almost knocking out the shelf behind me in the process. Thankfully, no one notices as I quietly right myself and take my spot next to Ivy.

When she glances at me, her cheeks are even more flushed than after a long ski run. Her chest heaves up and down, and my stomach twists. Did I make her uncomfortable? That's the last thing I wanted. When I pretended we were a couple, it was for the opposite reason. And now, I worry I messed everything up.

17

Stirring The Sauce

Ivy

Is it really hot in here, or is it just me? Gosh, I wish I'd worn something lighter than a sweater. Zane's body heat compounding with mine didn't help one bit, and I wish I could roll in the snow to cool down. I'm pretty sure vapor would sizzle out of me in the process.

Zane studies me with a deep frown, and I'm not sure if it's Giuseppe getting on his nerves or something else. He kind of looks worried, so I offer him a small smile.

Relaxing his shoulders, Zane returns his attention to Giuseppe. Our instructor is gesticulating wildly as he explains the rest of the recipe while our dough is resting. After the pressure and tension we just put it under, I understand why it needs some relaxation time.

"*Va bene*. We are going to cook the spinach." He says each word as if it ends with a hard "e." He punctuates every following word with his hands, and at this point, I'm starting to get dizzy.

I risk a glance at Zane. His jaw is clenched, and his lips pressed so hard they're turning white. Probably sensing my gaze, he looks at me, and the corner of his mouth twitches. I bite my lip to keep from laughing. That would be extremely rude. Giuseppe is nice, but he's just so extra.

I shake my head, pulling myself into focus as I listen to Giuseppe's instructions. Once he finishes, we get started on the spinach. To my utmost surprise, we're not terrible at this. Sure, it's a pretty basic recipe. I chose the "everyday cooking lesson" because I knew both my skill level and Dan's, and I just wanted us to have a nice moment together—not necessarily learn how to cook fancy dishes that we would never eat again. My stomach clenches at the reminder that I should be doing this with Dan, and guilt creeps in when I realize I'm not that upset it's Zane standing next to me instead. Actually, I think I prefer it this way. What's wrong with me? I was about to marry Dan. Even if he's the one who left, I should still be hung up on him, right? Why don't I feel that way, when he was still hung up on his ex after all these years?

Giuseppe's voice startles me again—I'm definitely not getting used to it—and we move on to the next element: the sauce.

It's all very easy to execute, and Zane and I make a good team. A better team than Dan and I would have made, for sure. Dan was more a sit-on-the-couch-with-a-beer-while-I-cook kind of guy, and he would have probably spent half the lesson checking his phone. But Zane looks relaxed, even if this is far from his usual scene. He's mixing the sauce slowly, like Giu explained, while I add the spices and herbs.

"Should we try it?" I suggest once everything is in the pan.

His eyes widen a little. "Moment of truth." He dips the spoon in the creamy sauce and brings it to my face, his over-serious display drawing a giggle out of me.

"Come on," he says. "The anticipation is killing me."

"Right." Blowing on the spoon, I taste some of the sauce from the end of it and close my eyes in delight. "It's *so* good."

He dips the spoon in the sauce again and tastes it for himself. The fact that he used the same spoon isn't lost on me and stirs something inside my chest.

"Mmm," he says. "You're right. We're good at this." Raising his hand, he gives me a high-five. "Guess it's a good thing I tagged along." He winks, and I bump my shoulder with his.

The other couples seem to be doing great—particularly Lina and Jude, who are a lot more organized and look like pros. Well, pros who can't keep their hands off each other. My stomach tangles in knots again. Even if I'd been here with Dan, I don't think we'd have been oozing happiness the way they do. Frankly, it never was our style. Our relationship was more a "comfortable" thing than a "sparks flying, eating each other with our eyes" kind of deal. And that thought hurts. What if I never find something like that?

"I'm stuffed," I say, leaning back in my chair and putting my fork down. We're seated at a round wooden table in the hotel restaurant, and we just finished devouring the ravioli we made. We're all sitting at different tables, and Giuseppe is back in the kitchen preparing a little "*sorpresa*" for us.

Zane pats his stomach. "That was a lot of food." Then, his voice drops to a whisper. "A lot more filling than the children I had earlier."

I giggle, shaking my head. "Well, they were only breakfast. This is lunch."

His smile widens, and it turns my insides to mush. "Right."

"*Amici*," Giuseppe exclaims, entering the room. "Here comes *il dolce*! The famous Italian tiramisu."

My eyes widen. If I eat anything else, I'm going to burst. Around us, everyone seems to agree with me, except maybe Marius, who looks eager.

"I know you didn't make this, but I couldn't let you leave without dessert, no?" Giuseppe says, placing a share plate on each of our tables, a large smile plastered on his face.

As stuffed as I am right now, I have to give this a try. First, because it would be rude not to since he made it just for us. Second, because Giuseppe is adorable, and we had a fantastic afternoon. Third, because, well, it smells amazing.

"I'm hungry again," Zane says, a confused frown etched on his face. "How can I be hungry again?"

I giggle, grabbing the spoon to serve us both. "I know. Me too."

The tiramisu melts on my tongue, and I moan in pleasure. "It's incredible."

Zane swallows his bite, looking at me before nodding. "Delicious."

"How do you like it?" Giuseppe asks, hands placed flat on our table.

"It's so good," I say. "I love how the bitterness of the coffee and cacao blends with the sweetness of the sugar. It's perfection."

"*Si*," he says, pinching his fingers before kissing the tip in a very "chef's kiss" way. "That's the beauty of the tiramisu. Two things that wouldn't go well on paper make the most unique and *perfetto misto di sapore*. Um . . . mix of flavors. A little like a couple," he adds with a wink before walking to the other tables.

Zane and I gaze at each other for a second, neither of us saying anything before we dig into the sumptuous dessert again and clean our plate.

After saying goodbye to the other couples and Giuseppe, thanking him for a great time, we leave the restaurant. I'm happy to get some fresh air again, and judging by the look on Zane's face, and the fact that he didn't even bother to put his coat on, I'd say he feels the same.

We meander down the street with no destination in mind, just taking a pleasant stroll through town. We don't talk, but it's not awkward or weird. It's more peaceful. The smell of hot cocoa and caramelized nuts overwhelm the crisp mountain air as we approach the Christmas market.

"Oh, gosh. I don't think I'll be eating for days," I joke, patting my stomach.

He coughs out a chuckle. "Same."

We keep walking until my feet feel so heavy, I need to sit down again. We settle into a bench overlooking the ice skating rink, where we watch the skaters glide across the ice, some more skilled than others.

Zane yawns loudly. "Sorry," he says. "I'm drained. Between Giuseppe's overwhelming personality and the indecent amount of food in my system, I have no energy left."

I yawn too. "Let's go ice skating then. We'll fall asleep right here on this bench if we don't do something."

His eyes widen just enough for me to admire the intensity of his gray irises. "Seriously?"

A large grin breaks onto my face. I kind of want to crash on my bed right now, but the idea of seeing Zane ice skate is just too good to pass up. "Oh, come on," I say, bumping my shoulder with his.

He arches an eyebrow and gives me a pointed look. "You've been cooking this up since yesterday, haven't you?"

"Please don't say cook," I say through giggles. "Are you in? It'll be fun."

"Fine." He rolls his eyes, springing to his feet. "Let's go *ice skating,* I guess."

I clap my hands. "Yay!"

We walk to the booth, where we rent two pairs of skates that Zane insists on paying for. And then, off we go. I have never skated before, but I'm sure it's not that difficult, right? Skiing actually looks like a sport, but skaters look like they're just gliding around peacefully.

Well, let me tell you something. There is nothing peaceful about me on ice skates. Not that I'm *on* that much. I barely take two steps on the ice before I look like the trembling baby deer from yesterday. But since I'm a grown woman and not a cute, tiny creature, it's not quite as charming.

Zane, of course, masters the art perfectly.

"You said you didn't like ice skating," I say, slightly out of breath, as he helps me up after yet another fall.

He shrugs. "I don't, but not because I'm bad at it."

I stick my tongue out. "You're so annoying."

He just smirks at me, gliding backwards and holding my hands to steady me.

After a few more laps, I feel more at ease, and I even dare to drop Zane's hands and skate off on my own. It's a lot like skiing, in a way. I just needed to find my balance.

I'm now on my bazillionth lap, and I'm finally feeling braver.

"Look," I tell Zane. "I'm as good as you now."

He chuckles, nodding in agreement, and I skate faster to show off my moves—except I have none. I stumble on literally nothing except my feet and reach for Zane's arm to avoid falling, but I drag him down with me. Somehow, I roll on my back, and my feet end up near Zane's face.

He lets out a low scream as I sit up.

"Are you okay?" I ask.

He sits up, his hand on his cheek. "Yeah, I'm fine."

But the moment he removes his hand, my stomach hardens, and it feels like I just drank a gallon of ice water. "Oh my gosh, Zane. You're bleeding."

18

Scars

Zane

"I'm fine," I reassure Ivy, who's still apologizing as a small crowd forms around us. "It's nothing."

"It's not nothing, Zane," she retorts, her pitch an octave higher than usual. "We have to get this cleaned up. You might need stitches."

I wave my hand in dismissal. "I'll just wash it out later." There's really no need to fuss over a little cut.

"It could get infected," Ivy says, worry written all over her face as we return our skates. "Don't you have a clinic in town?"

"There's one further down the street," I say. "But seriously, we don't need to—"

"We're going," Ivy says, her tone firm.

Releasing a low groan, I follow her, knowing it's pointless to argue with a nurse about first-aid care. We zoom down the street until we reach the small clinic.

And when I say small, I mean Winter Heights small, which is tiny. The clinic is a single rectangular room with two beds separated by a curtain along with a desk area, a back room, and a few waiting chairs. None of them are empty, and at least a dozen people are standing around.

"What on earth happened?" Ivy's eyes go wide as she takes in the sight. "Is there some kind of apocalypse we didn't know about?"

I shake my head. "They're just tourists." Visitors always do stupid stuff and end up getting injured. Well, I guess I'm just like them now. Definitely hitting an all-time low. It's because I went tubing. That's when it all started.

"Zane," says the nurse, Claire, as she approaches. "Are you—Ow, that's a nasty cut."

I arch an eyebrow. "Really? I barely feel it." I brush my cheek with my hand and touch the thickness of drying blood on my skin.

"It'll get infected if you don't clean it out soon," she says, coming closer to examine the gash. "You might even need sutures."

Ivy sighs. "Told you. I'm so sorry."

"Oh, hello there," Claire says, noticing Ivy. She's not as surprised as I would have expected, which can only mean one thing. My outings with Ivy are already the talk of the town.

"Hi, I'm Ivy," she says, sticking her hand out.

"I'm Claire, nice to meet you." She shakes Ivy's hand, then turns to me. "Well, grab a seat, and I'll be with you as soon as I can. Sorry. Today is mayhem."

"I can help, if you want?" Ivy offers. "I'm a registered nurse."

Claire glances at her, then at me. "Oh, you're so sweet. But I wouldn't want you to ruin your date. Just—"

"It's not a date," Ivy and I both blurt at the same time.

I clear my throat, suddenly feeling warm again. Why can't they have an outdoor clinic? It's always too darn hot inside.

"I'm here on vacation, and we're just, um, friends."

"Right. Well, you're on vacation. It wouldn't feel right to make you work."

"It wouldn't feel right to not help out," Ivy says with her warmest smile. "If I can do anything to ease the load, I'd be happy to. Either way, I'll have to wait for you to get to Zane. That way, it'll be quicker."

Claire casts me a quick glance, and I give her a nod. I don't know if Ivy is any good at her job, but I know she's a good person and wants to help. Claire clearly needs it.

"Thank you," Claire says with a wide smile. "Next patient is that kid over there with his mom. You'll find all the supplies we have available in the back. If you think they need to see a doctor, just have them wait. He'll be here in about an hour."

Ivy nods. "I'll wash my hands and get started."

I lean back against the wall and watch her work. It quickly becomes clear that she is, in fact, very good at her job. Patients' faces light up when they talk to her. She's efficient in everything she does and great with kids, playing games with them and making them laugh. She's even more beautiful now that she's immersed in her element. She tied her hair up in a ponytail, clearing her face.

"Your turn, big boy," she says as she saunters up to me, a hand on her hip.

"Already?" I glance around. Sure enough, only three other patients are here aside from the one Claire is treating.

"Yep. It was mainly just upper respiratory infections and cuts. Sit right here." She gestures to the examination table.

I sit down while she grabs the wheeled cart of supplies and snaps on a pair of blue latex gloves. "Let's clean this up."

I try to stay immobile as she cleans the wound on my cheek. Her touch is gentle, as I knew it would be.

"You'll be fine," she murmurs. "It looked deeper than it really is."

I throw her a pointed look. "Told you."

A smile tugs at her lips as she applies a small bandage. "Just make sure it stays dry. Change the bandage every day."

"Noted. Thanks for patching me up."

She chuckles, taking her gloves off and tossing them into the trash bin. "It's the least I can do after giving you a permanent scar."

"What?" I ask, eyes widening. "You said—"

Her eyes crinkle with laughter. "I'm kidding. You'll be fine. No lasting damage."

I press my hand over my chest dramatically. "Thank heavens."

After Ivy helps out with the last patients, I walk her back to her hotel. I'm racking my brain for something, anything, to extend our time together, but it's getting late. Everything is closing, and food is out of the question for the next twelve hours, minimum.

Too soon, her hotel comes into view.

"Thanks for walking me back," she says as we stop by the front entrance. "And sorry again for your cheek."

I wave my hand. "It's all right. I promise, I don't even feel it."

"You will have a scar, though—even if it'll go away after a while," she adds, wincing.

"Your way of making sure I don't forget about you when you're gone?" I ask, forcing a cocky smile.

"Absolutely," she says through a giggle.

As if I could forget her. Ever.

A silence falls between us.

I clear my throat. "Well, I'll get going, then. See you tomorrow morning for your lesson?"

She smiles warmly. "See you tomorrow, Zane."

Reluctantly, I turn to walk away, dragging my feet. Why does it have to be like this? Why does she have to be a tourist when she so clearly belongs here? The cold doesn't seem to bother her, she already knows plenty of townies, and her eyes sparkle every time she gazes up at the mountain. It's just not fair. Why did some moron have to go and break her heart? Why can't I be the one for her?

As I walk home, that last question plays on repeat in my mind, torturing me, as I'm sure it will the entire night.

Yup. Called it. All I could think about as I lay in bed was Ivy, and frustration took over as I mulled over this unbearable turn of events. Why did the Universe introduce me to Ivy if I can't be with her?

Feeling particularly grumpy today—even the extra cold shower didn't boost my mood—I step outside, relieved not to come across Daisy. The last thing I want right now is human interaction.

I walk to the barn, and my heart leaps at the warm welcome I receive from my dogs. This will never get old. I don't know how people can function without them.

"Hey, guys!" I say, entering the enclosure. Half of them come running, jumping up and licking me all over. I wrestle with Bobby, Blaze, and Bella before lying back on the hay.

Furry heads are all over me instantly, and I cuddle each of them in turn.

"Why can't my life be as easy as yours, huh?" I ask while scratching Bagel and Bean at the same time. "Going on rides, playing in the snow, eating, and sleeping. That's the dream life, right there." Especially if I got to do it with Ivy.

I keep cuddling them and wrestling with the rowdier ones until my batteries are fully recharged, and my mood is largely improved.

Finally, it's time for my lesson with Ivy. I get dressed, grab the keys for Darwin's hut, and head downtown.

She's already standing at the entrance when I arrive, wearing a new pair of ski pants, though she's still donning that annoying white-and-pink "Mrs." coat.

"Hey," she says, all sunshine and smiles. Usually, that would dampen my mood, but Ivy's smiles have a way of melting my insides faster than a cute puppy.

"Hey, how was your night?" I ask, setting her skis down in front of her.

"Good. Quiet. I went to bed early. Between all the food and the emotions, I needed some rest," she says with a chuckle.

A weird sensation of relief washes over me.

"And you?"

"Good," I lie. "Turned in early too." How about not at all?

"So, where are we going today?" she asks, sliding her skis on.

"Same as yesterday. You did great, but I want you to get used to the poles."

I give her a few more pointers, and off we go. We take a couple of drag lifts until we reach the chairlift, climbing up the mountain to the longest green run of the resort.

"This view never gets old," she breathes, looking around.

"It really doesn't. It's the only thing keeping me sane. And from eating young children," I add, glancing at her. I'm rewarded by one of her gorgeous smiles.

"Well, thank—"

The chairlift creaks to a stop. Ivy's eyes widen, and she cranes her neck back, trying to see what's happening.

"Don't worry, it's nothing," I say. "Someone probably fell at the bottom or the top, and they had to push the emergency stop button."

"Um, okay." She doesn't look reassured in the least. "We can't fall from here, right?"

"Not any more than when we're moving," I say, and her eyes widen further. "No. That means no. Just stay calm."

"Okay." There's a tense silence. "Do they send someone to get us if they can't get the lift started again? Would anyone even know? There's no cell service in this town."

I place a hand on her arm, giving it a little squeeze. "That won't be necessary. It'll likely start up in a few minutes. This actually happens a lot."

She nods, her eyes meeting mine.

"I have a landline, by the way. If you need to contact anyone. Your sister or anyone else."

She wrinkles her forehead, then shakes her head, her copper highlights catching the sun. "Oh, no, that's fine. We text a little when I'm on the hotel's wi-fi. She doesn't have much time to chat anyway. She's on vacation too."

"Oh, yeah? Where?"

"She and her fiancé are in Florida, actually. They don't get a lot of time off since they work in the restaurant business, but she's showing him around the state."

"Nice. But it's a shame they came to visit while you were away. You said you were close, and I'm guessing you don't see her a lot since she lives in Paris." I realize what I said the second the last word leaves my mouth, and I want to jump off the chairlift as punishment. But then Ivy likely *would* fall.

Her face tints. "They—"

"Sorry, it just came out. Forget it. Hey, let's talk about this gorgeous view again. My favorite peak is actually that one, right over there," I say, pointing to the far right.

She shakes her head vigorously. "It's fine, Zane. I need to get used to talking about this. Whether I like it or not, it's part of my life now. Hopefully, one day I'll be able to laugh about it. Yes, my sister and her fiancé *were* in town for my wedding. I did spend a few days with them, and I even got some alone time with my sister before the non-wedding. I'm crossing my fingers that I'll be able to visit Paris again in a few months."

Once again, I'm reminded how strong this woman is. And once again, I want to smash someone's head. Hard.

"This vacation has been good for me, you know?" She lets out a breath of vapor, fixing her gaze on the horizon. "I haven't had time to myself for a very long while, and seeing that younger couple yesterday at the cooking class made me realize that Dan and I never really had that."

I gulp. "Oh?"

"He was always working so much, and we honestly didn't have a lot in common. But he was nice and—I don't know—I thought that was enough. What I wanted. Only now, I'm starting to think I was just settling. Sure, it sucks to be back to square one at almost thirty, but it's a good thing, I think. I've never felt more myself than I have these past few days. When I was with Dan, I was always hiding behind him, letting him take the lead, but this trip gave me more confidence. Anyway," she says with a nervous chuckle. "Sorry. I'm rambling."

"I'm glad you're feeling better." *Glad* isn't exactly the right word to express what I feel. The fact that she's gotten over that jackass is everything to me. More than I'd hoped to hear from her. "You don't deserve what that jerk did to you."

"Thanks." Her smile pierces right through my chest.

We feel a little jolt, and the chairlift starts moving again.

Ivy lets out a sigh of relief that makes me chuckle. "And here I thought you were completely calm and collected."

She lets out a nervous giggle, eyes widening. "Nope, not even close. I can't wait to get out of this thing. I *am* more confident now, but in *myself*. Not in a suspended chairlift bench."

Her wish is soon fulfilled, and once we're off the lift, we ski down the long green slope without too much trouble. She does fall a couple of times, but it's more for lack of attention than skill.

We ski two more smaller slopes before heading down to the resort.

"Good work. You're really improving," I say, and her face lights up.

"Thanks. It was really fun. I think this was the first time I really enjoyed skiing, and it didn't feel like too much of a struggle."

"I'm glad. Skiing has always been one of my favorite ways to exercise my body and clear my mind."

"Yeah," she says, taking her skis off. "I wish I could do it on a regular basis. You're so lucky. Maybe I'll give water skiing a try when I get home. It's probably not as amazing, but it's the only sport that would come close."

My heart lurches at the reminder that Ivy's days here are numbered. "Yeah."

I hoist our skis on my shoulders, and we start walking toward the street. "Any activity planned for this afternoon?" I ask, craving more time with her.

"I have a mani-pedi at the spa this afternoon that I'm looking forward to, and then I'll do a bit of shopping. I haven't bought any souvenirs yet."

"Oh, cool." I clear my throat. "What about tonight? It's New Year's Eve, after all."

"Right. It'll be a quiet night for me," she says with a chuckle. "I'll have room service, but don't feel bad for me, because I have a whirlpool tub with a view of the fireworks."

"That's unacceptable." I shake my head, even though a night with Ivy in a hot tub sounds like heaven to me. "Come with me to a party."

I kind of blurted the words out without really thinking them over. But honestly, I would love for her to come with me. Sure, it'll most likely be a little awkward since I'm not exactly known for bringing girls to parties, and the entire town is probably talking about us already, but I'm desperate for as much Ivy time as I can get.

"I didn't pin you for the party type." She raises a dark-brown eyebrow.

"Okay. It's not exactly a Miami party," I joke. "It's more a get-together with some of the townies at my brother's house."

She bites her lip, and I'm pretty sure she's looking for a way to let me down gently. But then, her face lights up, and she says, "I'd love to."

19

New Year's Eve

Ivy

I've upturned my suitcase onto my bed, scouring the contents for a magical, stunning New Year's Eve-worthy outfit that might have sneaked its way in without me knowing. But alas, no luck.

I hate when that happens.

Instead, I grab a pair of black jeans and a black sweater with a peter pan collar embroidered with white pearls. It's not very fancy, but I doubt the party will be any fancier. At least I hope not. I'll add a bit of makeup, and that should do the trick. I'm gliding into the bathroom when someone knocks at the door. I put my makeup case next to the sink and hustle over to open it.

I squint through the peephole, and my heart thuds when I see Zane's large frame. He tilts his head a little, and I get a close-up of his bandaged cheek. I wince at the sight, then open the door.

"What are you doing here?"

His eyes widen, and a gleam flashes in his gray irises. "Hey, you look great."

I look down at my clothes. "Thanks."

"Sorry . . . that I came up here—and early," he says, clearing his throat. "I, um, didn't say anything about the dress code, and Daisy mentioned that I should have."

"Oh, well, is this okay?"

He swallows, his eyes trailing down my body. "Perfect."

I sigh. "Good, because I fought with my suitcase, but this is all I could find," I joke, opening the door to let him see the mess on my bed.

He cranes his head forward to look. "Ouch."

"Can you just give me one more second? I'll put some makeup on, and then we can go. You can come in."

"All right," he says, and as soon as he crosses the threshold, his fresh mountain scent takes over the room. I suddenly wish I could bottle it and use it as a candle or a room freshener. "Nice room," he grunts.

"I know," I say, heading to the bathroom. "I love it."

He whistles. "And you weren't kidding about that bathtub."

"You thought I was?"

He chuckles, but it sounds a little off. "Kinda."

"So what should I expect tonight?" I ask as I apply some mascara

"Are you nervous?"

My insides twist. Yeah, you could say that. It's not that I think I won't enjoy it, but this party thing feels a lot like a date thing, and it's making my head dizzy with questions. Do I want to go? Do I want to go with Zane? *Should* I want to go? Is it normal that I want to go? The list is endless.

As I'm applying my makeup, I say, "Well, it's always a little nerve-wracking to go to a party where you don't know anyone."

"You'll know me," he says, and I'm sure he's sporting a smirk right now. "Don't worry, everyone will love you. You're a very lovable person."

My heart pounds hard against my ribcage, and I swear it's going to pop out. I lean against the sink, enjoying the cold, soothing sensation on my stomach. "I am?"

"Yeah..." He clears his throat. "You know, for a tourist."

I laugh, and he joins me with a low chuckle.

I finish applying my mascara and join him in the main room. He's standing there, looking outside. Staying here in my room has never sounded so appealing.

"Are you ready?" he asks.

I shake myself out of my trance. "Yep."

After putting my coat and shoes on, I follow him out of my room.

During the walk to his brother's house, he fills me in on everyone's names, and I learn he also has a three-year-old nephew, Aaron. And with Belinda there, it looks like I'll be meeting his entire family tonight. Way to put pressure on a girl. Not that it means anything. We're just friends.

His brother's house is a wooden structure with a chalet vibe. Though it's a bungalow, there are a few steps leading to the front door. It's situated at the beginning of the street leading to Zane's farm. As we approach the front door, music streams out of the house, and my chest tightens.

Zane doesn't bother to knock and just barges right in. After taking off our coats, we follow a long corridor to a large living area, where about two dozen people are mingling, eating, and drinking.

"Brother," a large guy bellows, hobbling on crutches toward us. He immediately gives me teddy-bear vibes. The guy looks a lot like Zane, but his eyes are a warm shade of brown, and he oozes friendliness. Not that Zane isn't friendly—he is, but only once you get to know him. The man places both of his crutches in one hand to give Zane a side hug.

"Hey," Zane greets. "This is Ivy."

"Pleasure to meet you. I'm Darwin," the man says, smiling.

"Likewise. Thanks for having me over."

"Of course. Here's my son, Aaron," he says beckoning to a cute kid with dark hair who comes running toward us.

I talk with Darwin for a bit, but my eyes keep darting to Zane and his nephew. Watching him spinning Aaron in circles and making him giggle does weird things to my stomach. I know he's a good guy, and he's a lot warmer when you get a glimpse under those gruff outer layers, but every interaction he's had with kids since I met him are far from the joy that lights up his face when he's with his nephew.

Daisy joins us, along with Pete, Lea, and Marco, who live further down the street.

"Guys," Daisy says to the others, giving me a quick hug. "This is Ivy, Claire's savior and Zane's *friend*."

"Oh, right!" Marco raises his glass. "We heard about how you saved the day."

My cheeks heat up. "I hardly saved the day."

"Sure she did," Zane says, startling me. I didn't even know he was listening. "Ivy was great. Patched me up all nice." He turns his cheek to show off his bandage.

I shake my head, fighting a grimace. "Only because I hurt you in the first place."

He gives me a falsely annoyed look, then places a hand on my shoulder. "I'm fine."

The place he touches immediately erupts in flames, and the way Daisy's looking at the scene—like it's the first time in history that Zane has placed his hand on someone else's shoulder—doesn't help.

Zane pulls me away and introduces me to more people, and I even spot some familiar faces, like Shane from the ski lift, Ethan from the snowmobile place, and Seth, Zane's employee. We finally make it to the buffet, and the food is to die for.

Everyone I come across is so warm and welcoming, instantly putting me at ease. Darwin is quite the jokester, too, and he does a good impression of Robert De Niro. I'm really going to miss them all when I leave. It's a great community to live in.

"Ah, there you are," Zane says to someone behind me before shoving a spinach mini tart in his mouth and wiping his hands. I turn around to see a sixty-something lady wearing a red sweater and a beautiful golden husky brooch. This has to be Belinda.

"My boy," she says, patting Zane's cheek like a mom or a grandma would do. "I know I'm late. I didn't set an alarm for my nap, and that threw me off." She places a loud kiss on his uninjured cheek, and I'm pretty sure if it were anyone else, Zane would be groaning and wiping it off.

"I wanted to introduce you to Ivy," he says, turning to me.

I take a step forward and stick my hand out, but Belinda takes me into her arms, squeezing me tight. "It's wonderful to finally meet you. I've heard so much about you," she says into my hair.

Really? Zane talked to her about me? The thought sends a thrill through my belly.

"And you're a pretty good skater too, apparently," she adds with a small wink.

I freeze. Of course, that's how she heard about me. "Oh gosh," I say, burying my face in my hands. "I feel awful about that."

Zane places an arm around my shoulders, tugging me to his side. "Stop beating yourself up, Ivy. I'm okay."

I gulp, risking a glance at him. His magnetic eyes imprison me for a second, and all I can manage is a nod.

"He really is," Belinda chimes in. "He's a big boy."

"I am." Zane plasters a large grin on his face. "Do you want something to eat or drink?" he asks Belinda.

"A martini? And all the food I need is right here," she says, turning to the buffet.

"Anything for you?" he adds, looking at me.

I raise my glass of wine. "I'm good."

"You are absolutely gorgeous," Belinda says to me as soon as Zane leaves us. She takes a step back to study me, then rearranges my brown locks like a mother would.

A warm blush spreads on my cheeks. "Thank you."

"You know, Zane isn't really my son, but it certainly feels that way. Daisy, Darwin, they all feel like my children."

I nod. "That's wonderful." And I mean it. I'm so glad they had Bruce and Belinda while growing up. It seems like they really cared for them. Belinda still does.

"It truly is. So, believe me when I say this," she begins, helping herself to a cocktail sausage. "You must mean a great deal to Zane if he brought you here tonight. That boy doesn't open up easily."

"Oh, we're just friends," I stammer, my blush intensifying.

She shakes her head. "I've seen how different he's been these past few days. He's in a good mood, laughing, going on rides, coming home late."

"Oh, well. I don't kn—"

"*I* know," she says firmly. "He never talks to me about anyone, but the last two lunches we spent together, all he could talk about was you."

Casting her a faint smile, I tilt back the rest of my wine, but nothing will be enough to cool me down right now.

20

Fate

Zane

Being with Ivy here tonight feels right, natural. Like I've known her all my life. Just like I knew she would, she's getting along with my family. Even if I'm having a great time, this doesn't help with the way I feel about her. I never thought I'd ever want to be with someone again after what happened with Sofia. I was happily resigned to life as a lone wolf. But in the span of a few days, everything changed, and that scares the heck out of me.

I'm walking back to Belinda and Ivy when Darwin appears at my side. He places a hand on my shoulder.

"How's the knee?" I ask him.

"Still hurts. But it's getting better. The swelling has come down, so there's that. Hopefully, I'll get back on my feet soon." He moves to stand in front of me. "So, Ivy's great. I'm glad you're finally getting back out there, bro."

"I'm not."

He furrows his eyebrows.

"Getting back out there, I mean. She's just a friend."

"It doesn't look like it to me. Even Ethan said so. You guys look way too cozy to be just friends."

I release a long groan. I'm not sure whether it's because he's annoying me, or because I wish he was right. "Well, we are. She's leaving in a few days. There's nothing there."

"Of course. I'm not saying this has to be anything more. Just a little vacation fling." He winks. "Exactly what you need."

Could this *be* a fling? Do I even want a fling with Ivy?

"I need to get Belinda her drink," I grumble, moving past him. I don't want to talk or think about any of this now. Not when I know that whatever happens will inevitably lead nowhere.

Belinda and Ivy are laughing when I join them, and the sight makes my heart beat just a little faster.

"Thank you, my boy," Belinda says when I hand her the martini.

"Are you okay?" Ivy asks, cocking her head to the side to scrutinize me.

I scratch my beard. "Yes. It's—I'm going to go outside."

"Been cooped up for too long?" she asks with a smile.

"You know me," I joke, but the fact that she really does goes straight to my heart. How can someone I just met understand me so well? And not just about my craving the cold, but everything else. "Do you want to come?"

She nods. "Sure."

We grab our coats and step out onto the wooden deck at the back of the house. It stretches across three quarters of the house and was a pain to build. But now that it's done, I love hanging out here.

I take a deep breath and set my beer on the railing. It's dark out, but strings of colorful lights on the trees and beams illuminate the backyard.

"It's so pretty out here," Ivy says, pulling her gloves from her pocket.

"I know. Same view as when we were kids, but a whole different perspective."

She turns to me. "What do you mean?"

I sigh, my eyes roving the dark backyard. "This is my childhood home. Well, Darwin and I tore the old house down and rebuilt everything. But this right here is the land I grew up on."

"Wow, okay," she says, looking around.

A light chuckle escapes me. "If it wasn't for the yard, you wouldn't recognize it. It's the only part that hasn't changed. We spent so much time here, playing in the snow, climbing trees. It's always been my escape. Darwin's too. Our dad hated the outdoors and the cold. Inside the house, with his bottle in hand, was his favorite spot. So as kids, we would spend a lot of time outside."

"I'm sorry about your dad," she says, placing her hand on mine. "Did he—?"

"Die?" I glance at her, and the empathy in her eyes warms my entire body. "I don't know. Maybe. He always had a problem with alcohol. One day, he just packed up and left, and we never saw him again."

"I'm sorry." She squeezes my hand. "It's a good thing you had Bruce and Belinda to help you. She's so nice."

I smile. "I'm glad you like her. She really is a mother figure to us, just like Bruce was a terrific substitute dad."

She gazes out at the backyard again. "Well, it's a beautiful place to grow up."

"I'm sure Fort Lauderdale was too. I've never been, but you have gardens and nature there, don't you?" At least, I'd assume so.

She swats my hand, pulling hers away, and I instantly miss the contact. "Of course we do. It's just not as picturesque as the wilderness here. Not as peaceful . . ."

"It probably has its own beauty. You're just used to it by now."

"Yeah, maybe." She bites her lip. "So, it's almost midnight," she says. "Do you have any resolutions?"

I take a swig of my beer. "I don't do resolutions, since I know I'll never follow them," I joke. "I have no self-discipline."

She cocks her head to the side. "Oh, come on. I'm sure that's not true."

"It is." I nod. "I keep talking about expanding my business, but I never do."

"That sounds fun. What would you do?"

I roll my eyes, but honestly, I'm touched that she's taking an interest. "Just offer some hiking, camping, longer rides with ice-fishing excursions. That sort of thing."

"Those are all great ideas," she says, her face lighting up.

"Thanks. I actually used to offer camping and hiking in the summer, but I didn't this year . . ." I swallow hard at the reminder of how I spent my summer.

"Why not?"

I shrug. "A bad breakup, I guess. Messed me up pretty bad. Am I less of a man for admitting that?" I say it like it's a joke, but that's only half true.

She locks her beautiful green eyes on me. "That makes you *more* of a man, in my book. You're human, and you have emotions. Being a man or a woman has nothing to do with that."

"Yeah, I guess . . ."

She stares at the contents of her drink. "What happened?"

My first instinct is to cut this conversation short. The last thing I want is to talk about Sofia. Especially with Ivy. But I know she's not prying. She's been pretty open about her own heartbreak, so it's only fair I do the same. If there's anyone who can understand the feeling, it's her. Though I'm pretty sure her pain is a million times worse than mine. I never made it to the altar.

I lean my elbows over the railing. "Her name was Sofia. She moved here from Seattle to work during the high season, and we started seeing each other. We were friends before we got together, so I lost both when she left." My stomach constricts when I recall that moment she left—and all the moments after that. I spent the entire summer and fall sulking, not wanting to do anything except hang out with my dogs in the barn. I even avoided going on rides when the first snow finally came. Until Ivy.

"Why did she leave?"

"She didn't like it here. After two years, she decided she missed city life. Just when I was getting ready to propose."

Her mouth forms a small "o". "And you didn't want to go with her?"

"I'm a mountain guy," I joke, even though my insides are twisting. "Can you picture me in a city? I've never even left Colorado. All my family is here, my job, my dogs." Even if I did love Sofia, leaving this place was never in the books for me, and she knew that. But she decided she loved city life more than she loved me.

She looks down. "Yeah. I get it."

"But I'm better now. I feel like I'm finally back to normal. Time heals all wounds, I guess."

"Yeah. And you know what? It's her loss. You're a great guy, Zane Harden. I'm sure you'll find someone else who makes you happy."

The image that pops into my head is one of Ivy and me. I try to shove it away, but it keeps creeping back in. "You too," I mutter, feeling bile rising in my throat. Picturing her with someone else is torture. But I know she will find someone. Once her heart has healed, and she's open to dating again, she's going to make a lucky guy very happy.

"Thanks."

A silence falls between us, and I wonder if her mind is also reeling, imagining what our futures could look like.

"It's beautiful," she says in a breath, surprising me. I follow her gaze to the sky. It's particularly clear tonight, with hundreds of twinkling stars.

"It is." But I'm not looking at the stars anymore. Ivy's eyes sparkle brighter than the stars above us, drawing mine to hers like a magnet. She must feel my gaze on her, because she turns to me.

"Do you believe in fate?" she asks. "Like there's something written in the stars, and no matter what we do to fight it, it'll still happen?"

I swallow to wet my dry throat. "Maybe. I know there are things we don't understand. I know some things are impossible to push away, no matter how hard we try." Like those images inside my head, tormenting me.

"Exactly."

Her coat is now touching mine, and I don't know whether she took a step sideways, or if I did. Maybe it was both of us.

"Ivy," I say, grazing her cheek tenderly before pulling my hand away.

She takes it in hers, squeezing my palm, and my heart pounds faster than it ever has.

She leans toward me, and I know I can't back out. There's no way, when all I want is right here. I'm not strong enough to fight this. I need to feel her lips on mine.

Ivy's mouth parts at the same time as mine, and we're now inches from each other.

Then, a loud boom reverberates through the sky. Ivy jumps, and I raise my eyes to the fireworks crackling above us.

"It's midnight," I say, turning back to her, but she's already taken a step back. The spell is broken.

My friends and family start to fill the deck to watch the fireworks, shouting "Happy New Year" and taking me in their arms.

Ivy's expression is impossible to read. Is she glad we were interrupted? Should I just take her inside and finally kiss her, or should I give her space?

I try to find an answer in her eyes, but I can't. Offering a faint smile, she raises her head back to the fireworks that are lighting up the sky above us.

If I make only one resolution this year, it's to stop being a coward and go after what I want, because it's suddenly crystal clear.

21

Tender Loving Care

Ivy

I was so close to kissing Zane last night. The starry sky, the shimmer of holiday lights, the way he gazed at me. Everything was perfect, even the fireworks that ended up ruining the moment. But maybe it's for the best. Maybe the fireworks know better.

The only resolution I should make for this new year? Stay single.

After I take a shower and get dressed, I try calling Hazel one more time, but still no luck. How can this town operate here with so little service? Then, a light bulb goes off in my head. Zane mentioned a landline.

Glancing around the room, I spot the phone on the corner desk. Hastily, I type my sister's number and put it on speaker.

"Hello?" she says with her polite "I don't know who you are" voice.

"Happy New Year," I shout, even though we already exchanged well wishes via text.

"Ivy! Happy New Year. How are you? Whose number is this?"

"My hotel room. I just figured out they had a landline here." I shake my head. "But I'm good. How about you?"

"Great. We're actually in line at Universal Studios right now."

"Oh, hitting the park on New Year's Day? Big move."

"Yup. Surprisingly, it's not crowded at all. The park was basically empty when the gates opened. Now, a few more people are trickling in, but we're waiting in line for Hagrid, and it's only a thirty-minute wait."

"Wow. Unheard of."

"Exactly," she laughs. "So, how was your party last night? Did you have fun? Did you kiss the hot instructor at midnight?"

"Oh, shut up. It was great. The town even had fireworks at midnight. But no, I didn't kiss him."

My mouth dries when the words leave my mouth.

"But you wanted to," she insists, her voice teasing.

"No!" The lie has my cheeks instantly bursting into flames.

"Oh yes you did." She giggles. "I can tell. Even from however many miles away we are."

I sigh. "Exactly my point."

"Wait. *That's* your problem? You didn't kiss him because he lives in another state?"

I bite my lip. "Well . . ."

"Ivy. Why are you always so invested in every relationship you pursue? Couldn't you just have a little fling? Something to make your heart race and make you feel pretty while you're on vacation. There's nothing wrong with that."

"I don't do flings." Never have. I'm proud to be a relationship kind of gal. A fling isn't good for anything except breaking hearts. At least for me, because I don't know how to be with someone before handing them my heart on a platter with a big sign that says "crush it."

"Think of it as your new year's resolution, then," she peeps.

"Come on, Hazel. What girl kisses another guy a week after she was supposed to get married?" Guilt creeps back in, and I hate that it's still there.

"Ivy, the keywords in that sentence are '*supposed to.*' Do you think Dan and what's-her-face are playing chess right now?"

"I know, but it's different..."

"Why? Because you're the girl? Trust me, you have even more reason to be all over another guy right now. You deserve it."

I sink into the couch, hugging the pillow I beat up the other day. "It'd only mess everything up."

"New resolution," she says again. "Oh, I've got to go. We're up next. Love you."

"Okay. Have fun. Love you too."

As I hang up, I release a long breath. Could I really just have a fling with Zane? It's probably what he's looking for anyway, but am I even interested in that?

The image of Zane leaning in to kiss me plays over and over in my mind, sending shivers of anticipation down my spine and replacing the heartache of being dumped the night before my wedding. What I told Zane on the chairlift is true. After spending some time here, I no longer think Dan was the one. He never made me feel what I feel when I'm with Zane. The way my heart pounds when our bodies touch, the flutter in my belly that's triggered by a single one of his smiles, my mouth going dry when I lose myself in the depth of his gray eyes. As guilty as those things make me feel, I can't deny their existence, nor the fact that the only man I think about, all day and night, is Zane Harden.

After brunch, I mentally prepare for my ski lesson, trying to retrieve everything Zane taught me from my foggy brain. As soon as I spot him walking toward me with all the equipment hoisted on his shoulders, I forget all about snowplows and turning with poles. All I want to do is jump at him, wrap my arms around his neck, and kiss him.

"Hey," he says, a wide grin lighting up his face. "Sleep well?"

"I did." In fact, I wish my alarm clock hadn't gone off. Zane was in my dreams last night, and we weren't interrupted by the fireworks this time. "And you?"

"Not bad. Ready for your lesson?" He slides his skis on. "I want to try a blue run today."

My eyes widen slightly. "Already?"

"Yup. I think you can handle it."

I bite my lip, hesitating. "Okay. Let's just hope I won't start the year with a broken leg."

He chuckles. "I won't let that happen."

We ski down a few green slopes first so I can get my footing, and I feel a lot more at ease than before. We ski the whole slope without having to stop, and I have yet to eat snow today.

It's a clear day too, which helps with visibility. The perfect blue sky doesn't have a shadow of a cloud. Once we reach the top of the blue run, we pause to take in the view. It's steeper than any other slope I've tackled, but I'm not really scared. I trust Zane. He wouldn't take me here if he didn't think I could handle it.

"Ready?" he asks, putting his sunglasses on.

I nod. "Absolutely."

He flashes a bright smile. "Just be extra careful. It is a little crowded, and hangover tourists are a bigger hazard than usual."

I clear my throat, arching my eyebrow even though he can't see it behind my sunglasses.

He shakes his head. "You don't count as a tourist anymore."

My heart warms. It's silly, but the fact that Zane sees me as one of his own sends tingles through my body. Like I'm now a member of a super select club. And with Zane at the head, invites are probably tough to get.

"Just follow me, okay?" he says, a hand on my shoulder. "You'll do great."

"Yeah." I nod. "Let's do this."

And off we go. The blue slope really is crowded, but I focus on the techniques I learned and always stay in Zane's lane. He cranes his neck to throw me glances a few times, just to see if I'm still following, and I'm so proud to be doing this great. We stop twice, but not because I fall—just some quick breaks to enjoy the view.

Zane claps his hands when we slide to a stop at the bottom of the slope. "I'm impressed. That was excellent."

"Thank you." I beam, taking my sunglasses off. "Looks like I'm not too old for this after all," I joke.

"You're perfect . . ." he says, his gaze so intense it could melt the snow off this entire mountain.

"Anyway." I clear my throat, taking my skis off. "I have to get going. I have another massage session scheduled for this afternoon, and this time, I'm not bailing. After five days here, I really need some TLC."

Bending down to grab my skis, I bring them together and stand back up to hand them to Zane.

Only he's watching me with a pointed look. "Ahem."

"What?" I frown, struggling to fight my smile.

"You made me tag along for cooking class. I went ice skating and tubing with you. *Tubing!* And you don't invite me to the spa? That's just mean."

I burst into laughter, my cheeks burning up at the idea of Zane in a bathing suit. "You want to come to the *spa*? It's indoors, you know."

He wrinkles his nose. "I think I'd survive. You're not the only one who needs TLC once in a while."

"You're more than welcome to join me."

My heart rattles in my chest. I'm not sure if it's from the shock of Zane being willing to come, or the fact that he's the one who asked to join me. At the spa, of all places. Where we'll be in a warm environment with hardly any clothes on when we're used to hanging out with *more* layers than usual. Plus, I'm pretty sure it's not his scene—at all—and the thought of him stepping out of his comfort zone again just to spend time with me sends all kinds of butterflies tickling my belly. Yeah, that's definitely what makes my heart rattle the most.

22

Natural Habitat

Zane

The spa is not my scene. I've never actually been to one, but on paper, it's everything I despise. Indoors. Warm. People. Daisy actually *snorted* when I told her where I was going, and I didn't have any retort. Because snorting was the appropriate answer.

We stroll into the spa lobby that's decorated in limestone and dark wood paneling. A seating area with comfortable-looking couches and armchairs is on the left, and on the right, there's a reception counter framed by a couple of tall plants. I can already feel myself getting stifled by the stuffy atmosphere, which is enhanced by the incense they're burning and the zen music playing on the speakers. And in the span of a nanosecond, I just went from nervous to completely uncomfortable. Must be a new record.

We are greeted by a blonde receptionist I don't know. Probably a seasonal employee.

"Hi," Ivy says. "We have a reservation at five for a couple's massage. My name is Ivy Clark, but it might be under Ross."

The receptionist types on her keyboard for a moment. "Right. I see it here. The honeymoon special."

Ivy's face reddens, and her body tenses. "Oh n—"

"Yes, that's right," I say, putting my arm around her. The side of her mouth tilts up in an awkward grin, and she throws me a grateful glance. "I'm Zane, her husband." I don't mind pretending again. It's nothing compared to the pain she must endure every time she has to explain her situation.

"Right," Ivy says, leaning against me.

"Perfect. Well, the changing rooms are right here," the receptionist says, pointing to a couple of doors behind us, "and you can use the facilities before and after your treatment. Enjoy."

"Thank you," we both say, and she hands us some robes, slippers, and towels.

"See you on the other side," Ivy murmurs, retreating into the women's changing rooms.

With a deep breath, I head into the men's area. The space is empty, but it still feels way too small for some reason. Rows of lockers line both sides of the room, with benches in the middle. I make quick work of my clothes, throw them in a locker, and put the robe on. It's a little short, ending right under my knees, and the sleeves stop awkwardly a good three inches from my wrists.

When I step into the spa, it takes me a few seconds to adjust to the low lighting. A couple of fireplaces host roaring fires. Other than that, the only lighting comes from tiny LEDs on the ceiling that are clearly on the "warm" setting. A bunch of loungers and couches frame a sprawling rectangular pool, where a couple is swimming. At the far corner is a separate hot tub, a set of showers, and a sign that says "Hammam" and "Sauna" with an arrow pointing to a corridor. On my left is a long hallway, and right before it, a seating area with couches. Musky steam is wafting from a few conic diffusers at each corner of the room. The whole atmosphere is stuffy, hot, and humid—just like I imagine Florida would be. But for some reason, I don't *hate* it. It's just different, foreign.

The door to the women's changing room opens, and Ivy steps out in her bathrobe, her hair tied in a messy bun. Where my robe is clearly too small for me, hers is a little big. She had to roll up her sleeves, and the hem of the robe lands at her ankles.

"Should we try the pool first?" she whispers, nodding toward the water.

"Sure," I say in my normal voice.

She stifles a giggle. "Shh!"

Right, people are relaxing. Let's add the *whispering* requirement to the list of why this place isn't my element.

I feel like I'm being extremely noisy as we make our way to the loungers, even though I'm trying my best to tread quietly. But my slippers squeak with every step, and my heart pounds loudly in my ears.

But that's nothing compared to the way it rattles when Ivy takes off her bathrobe, draping it neatly on the lounger. I try to force myself not to look, but I can't. My eyes are instantly drawn to her body. She's wearing a one-piece black bathing suit, but the way it clings to her skin sends a prickling sensation through my whole body.

She turns to look at me, and I quickly avert my eyes, taking off my own robe. And I might be going crazy, but as I put it down, I feel Ivy's gaze raking my body the same way mine swept hers just seconds before.

We walk to the pool and step inside using the stairs. The water is warm, way too warm for my taste. But with every step, my body relaxes, and I begin to enjoy the soothing sensation it brings.

We paddle slowly to the other end, and I stop beneath a large cascade jet. The water splashes loudly on my shoulders, relieving the tension. Okay, maybe I could get used to this.

Ivy sits in the hot tub corner of the pool, and I join her.

"So," she says softly. "How's your first impression of the spa?"

I laugh way too loudly, even though I was going for a casual, light chuckle. "I like it," I whisper as best I can. "A little warm, but it feels nice."

"Right?" She closes her eyes, extending her arms along both sides, clearly enjoying the touch of the water.

Damn, this woman is beautiful. The way her messy bun secures her brunette hair gives me a clearer look at her flawless face. She's not wearing any makeup, yet her skin looks smooth, and the slight flush of her cheeks is exquisite. Absolute perfection, inside and out. I can't comprehend how every single person who gets to know Ivy doesn't fall in love with her instantly. Well, maybe they do. Maybe she left behind a trail of broken hearts before someone finally managed to crush hers. I still don't get how that moron could have done that. But even if it might sound cruel, I'm glad he left her. I'm glad she didn't settle for that prick and marry someone who clearly didn't deserve her.

We soak in the jacuzzi area for another ten minutes or so before heading to the sauna. We barely step foot in the warm room before I feel my chest constrict. An old man is lying down on a bench, perfectly still. I wonder for a second if he's breathing, until I see his chest rising ever so slowly. What's wrong with these people? How can this be how they relax?

Ivy sits, looking at me with a slight frown, and I scrunch my eyebrows in response. "Sorry. I can't," I whisper before getting the heck out of this death chamber.

Once I reach the pool area, I take a deep breath, only it's spoiled by that musky essential oil thingy. I dart to the shower area and set it to cold before stepping under the shower head.

I almost moan in relief.

"There you are." Ivy's voice chimes through the loud water crashing on my shoulders. "Are you okay?"

I turn the water off and give her an apologetic look. "Sorry. It's way too hot for me in there. I'd melt."

She bites her lip, a hazed look on her face. "Yeah . . ."

"You can go, though. I'll wait for you out here. I'd hate to ruin it for you."

She waves her hand in dismissal. "No problem. I've always preferred the hammam, anyway. I'm a Floridian. I like my heat more humid," she jokes.

"Do they have a snow room? That'd be more my vibe."

She chuckles. "They do, actually. Usually, after the sauna or hammam, you go into the ice room and rub ice all over your body."

I balk. "And you call that relaxation? This is insane."

"Well, said like that, it does sound kind of crazy," she says, her green eyes twinkling. "Do you want to try it? I'm not usually a fan, but I'll do it with you."

"Yeah, okay," I say, because those are the only words I want to say to Ivy. I don't want to be like her dumb ex-fiancé.

We go into the hammam, and it's absolute torture. There's so much steam filling the room, I can barely see anything. Which sucks, because the best part of doing stuff with Ivy is watching her enjoy herself.

"Are you okay?" she says after a few minutes.

"Yeah." I nod, steeling myself. I can do this. Besides, I'll be rewarded by the snow afterwards. Ivy stands up and grabs a glove from a box I didn't even notice. "What are you doing?"

"I'm going to scrub myself," she says. "The steam opens up our pores, and rubbing your body with a horsehair glove takes away all the dead skin. Try it"

"Isn't that a little unsanitary? To use the same glove."

She chuckles as she starts rubbing the glove on her leg. And just like that, the temperature rises again. I didn't even think that was possible. "They're single-use. When you're done, you put them in the trash outside."

"Oh." I bob my head in understanding. Grabbing one of the gloves, I mimic Ivy's movements, though mine are a little less graceful. Not to mention the exercise itself is making me sweat like crazy.

Finally, Ivy announces that we can go, and I practically run out of the hammam. She chuckles, and suddenly, all that torture was worth it because she looks happy, relaxed, and I'm glad I got to do that for her.

"All right, let's get you back into your natural habitat," she jokes.

"Yes, please."

We walk to the ice room, which is really just a small, open room with ice dripping from the ceiling into a large bucket. Ivy plunges her hands into the bucket and rubs ice on her arm, shivering in the process.

"Come on, big boy. Don't let me suffer on my own," she calls out.

All right. Let's do this. As unappealing as it sounds, I'm sure it's more bearable than sitting in the sauna or hammam. I imitate Ivy's moves and rub ice over my arms and thighs. To my surprise, it's not that bad. Once the initial sting passes, it's actually kind of soothing, numbing.

After a few seconds, she lets out a growl of frustration. "I can't anymore." She scurries out of the room, grabbing her robe and enveloping herself in it.

"Oh, really?" I say, rubbing my stomach. "I could do this all day."

A laugh bursts out of her. "Now who's insane?"

I keep going for a few more minutes. Eventually, even I start to feel chilled, so I get out and dry myself with the towel before putting my robe on.

"Should we just go to the waiting room and hang out there before our treatment?" she asks, checking her watch. "It's in fifteen minutes."

I nod, following her to the reception area where another essential oil diffuser awaits and the zen ambience music seems a notch louder. Ivy grabs a glass of cucumber water, offering me some, but I only drink my water straight.

There's no one else here, I realize as we sit down on the couch. I take a moment to reflect on the insanity happening right now. I, Zane Harden, am in a spa, about to undergo a treatment with the most gorgeous girl on the planet. All of this feels completely off, yet so right at the same time. It's so far detached from my normal life that somehow, it makes sense. It's as if this is where I have to be. Fate. Like Ivy said, sometimes things are out of our control. And if there's one thing I'm sure of, it's that I'd never be here if fate wasn't involved somehow, steering me.

"Wait," I say with a hint of worry. "It's not a hair removal thing, is it?"

She chokes out a laugh. "What? Of course not. It's a massage."

"Just checking. I know city men are a little different from regular men," I mumble, but it sounds more like a grunt.

She chuckles again, her eyes settling on me. "Scared of a little pain, Harden?"

My eyebrows shoot up. "Oh, that's not pain. That's *torture*."

"Tell that to every girl on the planet who has to shave before going on a date."

I shake my head. "I'd tell them to quit doing it. Nature is beautiful, and no one should suffer like that."

"Amen to that," she says, raising her paper glass.

"So, I was thinking," I begin, not really sure how to play this except straightforwardly. "Would you like to go snowshoeing with me tomorrow afternoon? It could be fun. A way to experience the mountain in a different way."

Her beautiful lips curl into a smile. "Sure, I'd love to."

"Great. I have the equipment and everything. We can go after our lesson." I kind of want to press further and ask her to lunch, but I don't want to push it. That would sound way too much like a date, and that's not what I'm going for.

Two masseuses wearing beige uniforms stride out from the corridor, and after confirming that we're indeed the lucky honeymoon couple, they take us to a double cabin where they ask us to undress and put on a tiny pair of plastic underwear. Then, they leave us alone to change.

I hold the skimpy object with the tip of my finger. "Yeah, there's no way I'm putting that on—or that it'll even fit."

Ivy barks out a laugh, shaking her head. "Men. You're all the same."

"Just saying it as it is. Not to mention, this thing looks incredibly uncomfortable."

She scrunches her nose. "You're not wrong about that. You can keep your bathing suit on. I have to change since I'm wearing a one-piece. Um, can you turn around?"

Heat bubbles in my chest. "Yeah, of course."

I turn the other way and try not to dwell on the fact that Ivy is undressing right behind me. Instead, I focus on how the cold ice felt on my skin earlier.

"I'm done," she says after a moment. When I turn around, she's already lying on her stomach, her body draped in the large, fluffy towel.

I do the same, and soon after, the masseuses knock and enter the room to begin our treatment.

They let us choose our essential oil for the massage, and I go with pine because it seems fitting.

The massage therapist's pressure is firm, but nowhere near strong enough that I can really feel it. She asks me a couple of times how it is, and I ask for more pressure. But the third time, I say it's better. Poor girl. I don't want her to break her arms working on me.

Suddenly, the door opens and closes in a whoosh. I don't pay too much attention to it, but then, whispers fill the room. I turn my head to glance at Ivy, who's clearly also wondering what's going on.

Just when I'm about to ask, my masseuse says softly in my ear, "I'm sorry, sir. But there is an urgent call for you."

23

Bobby

Zane

It takes me a second to register what the masseuse just said.

I shift my position and bolt upright. "A call for me? Where?"

Ivy's sitting up too, covering herself with her towel. "What's going on?"

"I'm not sure," I say, jumping off the table. "I'll be right back."

My heart pounds harder with every step. Who could be calling me? It must be important if they chased me down to Winter Heights' most luxurious hotel.

The spa assistant hands me a phone that's tucked away in a little office, then steps back through the door, closing it behind her.

"This is Zane."

"Zane!" Daisy's panicked voice comes through, and all the blood drains from my face. "It's Bobby. He's vomiting and drooling. He doesn't want to move. Something's wrong."

Adrenaline shoots through my system, and my heart stutters. "I'm on my way."

When I exit the room, Ivy's there, waiting for me. She's wearing her bathrobe, a concerned look on her face. "Zane. What is it?"

"It's Bobby. He's sick. I don't know." I rake a hand through my hair. "I have to go. Sorry."

"I'm coming with you," she says, falling into step beside me, and my heart skips another beat.

"You don't have to. You shou—"

"I'm coming." Her tone is firm, and the way she looks at me tells me there's no room for debate.

We change back into our clothes at lightspeed before practically sprinting to the farm. Dammit. Thousands of scenarios flash through my mind as we jog up the hill. I should have been more careful. He probably ate something he shouldn't have. He's always sneaking out and chewing on stuff. I found a few piles of vomit this week, but I thought it was nothing. The dogs often vomit because they eat too much or too fast. It's not that out of the ordinary. And anyway, there's no way to know who did it unless you catch them in the act.

Finally, my farm comes into view, and I barge into the barn. Seth and Daisy are kneeling next to Bobby, who's lying on his side, panting. He lifts his head when he sees me, then lays it back down, wailing.

The sound shatters my heart into a thousand pieces.

I drop to my knees, petting his head. "Boy, what's going on?" I examine his teeth and his tongue, which seems a little swollen.

"I'm taking him to Luke," I say once I finish my assessment. We need to run more tests. "Did you get a sample of his vomit or feces? Luke might need that to figure out what's going on. I'll get the car."

"I've got it," Seth says, handing me a plastic bag.

Daisy takes it first. "I'm coming with you."

I glance at Ivy, who's standing behind me with a worried expression. "No need. Ivy's coming."

"I am," she agrees, holding her hand out for the bag.

"Call Luke, and tell him we're on our way," I instruct Seth, who runs back to the house.

After bringing the car around and hauling Bobby into it, we rush to the vet, which is about thirty minutes down the mountain pass. I try not to think of everything that can go wrong in that timeframe, instead focusing on the road, traveling just a notch over the speed limit.

"He's going to be okay," Ivy says, still holding Bobby's vomit bag as she contorts herself to pat him in the back seat. He wails again, and my entire body constricts.

I grip the wheel harder, but I'm unable to form a reply. I've never lost a dog. Some have been injured, but it was always minor. I'm very cautious about their health. Bruce created a health schedule, and I've been following it scrupulously. Though not closely enough, apparently.

Finally, we pull up in front of the vet clinic. I jump out of the car. The front door swings open, and Luke's large figure appears with a stretcher.

"How is he?" Luke asks, furrowing his eyebrows.

"No change. I've been racking my brain, but the only plausible explanation is some kind of bacteria. You know how he loves to chew random stuff."

Ivy gives Luke a small wave, and he nods to her. Then, the three of us hoist Bobby out of the car and onto the stretcher.

Once inside, Luke asks me a battery of questions about Bobby's habits lately, and he examines him thoroughly before drawing his blood. He asks his assistant to take the sample to the lab immediately.

"I don't think it's a bacteria or a bacteria-induced disease. You said he's been eating a lot lately and that he's vomited a couple of times this week already."

"Yeah. In retrospect, I think it was all him. You know how it is. We can never be sure." I pat Bobby's head. "I should have taken him in sooner."

Ivy rubs my back to comfort me.

"I'm not saying it's your fault, Zane. Just trying to figure things out. If pet owners took their pets to the clinic every time they vomited, they'd be popping in every week."

Especially with Bobby, who likes to eat whatever he can find and then throw it up. Or half my dogs, for that matter. But still.

He makes Bobby swallow a charcoal tablet and palpates his abdomen at different places. As he does, Bobby's wails fill the room. He even tries to climb off the table despite his weakened state.

"It could be IBD. That's pretty common in Siberian huskies."

"Inflammatory bowel disease?" Ivy asks, frowning. "I didn't know dogs could have it."

Luke cocks his head. "Are you a doctor?"

"Nurse."

"Ah," he says, glancing between the two of us. "Well yes, they can. Especially huskies. It's a common immune disorder that affects the breed."

"Dammit," I hiss, walking away and raking a hand through my hair. "What does that mean? What do we do?" I've been extremely lucky that none of my dogs have had it until now.

"I can do an exploratory surgery to see if I'm right. Or I could give him more charcoal in case it's some kind of intoxication, and we can wait a few hours for his results to come in."

"Let's just do the surgery," I say, not wanting to lose any time. I don't care how much it costs. "I want to know now so we can figure out how to help him."

"Okay. After the surgery, I'll still need to send the sample to the lab, but Kathryn will get me the results in a few hours. I'll go prep now."

"Whoa. That's fast! And at this hour," Ivy marvels once he leaves the room.

I pet Bobby's head again. "Kathryn's his sister."

"Ah, that explains it. Good," she says, joining me in petting him. "IBD is not that bad. Not ideal by any means, but it's manageable. Usually, a new diet and some medication help with the symptoms."

When I raise my head, she's still petting Bobby with love. That's when it hits me just how lucky I am to have her in this situation. She's on vacation, yet she dropped everything to come here with me, held a bag full of dog vomit, and now, she's stroking Bobby and trying to make me feel better. She's truly an angel, dropped right from heaven. Or brought here by fate.

"Thank you," I say, struggling to get the words out, "for being here. You didn't have to come."

"Of course I did. I'm your friend." A warm smile spreads on her lips, bringing with it a hint of comfort. "And besides, I'm a nurse. It's what I do."

Friends. That word sends both a tingle of joy to my stomach and a slap to my face. But in the end, that's what she is. A friend who's here on vacation, healing the wound her stupid ex-fiancé inflicted. "I know, but still. Thanks."

"Don't mention it. Plus, Bobby's been my favorite since day one," she says with a chuckle.

A smile pulls at my lips. "Oh yeah, I remember. His tongue was all over your face."

"What can I say?" She shrugs. "We have a thing."

The fact that I'm even smiling at a moment like this shows how big of an impact Ivy has on me. I'm definitely starting to think *we* have a thing. But I don't mind sharing some of that Ivy magic with Bobby. He needs it right now.

24

The Hardest Thing

Ivy

It feels like hours have passed since Luke took Bobby into surgery. Zane is sitting next to me, his leg bouncing up and down as he stares into space. I want to say something to soothe his nerves, but I've been around patients whose loved ones were in surgery. There is nothing to say. All I can do is be here for him, even if the silence looms over us like a sword of Damocles.

He gets up, paces around the room, then sits back down. He drops his elbows to his knees while muttering something under his breath.

I rub circles on his back, and he lifts his face, throwing me a clouded look. His gray eyes seem to go through three different shades, and I must be a terrible person, because as we lock eyes, all I want to do is lean forward and kiss him. What's wrong with me? This man is in pain. It's neither the place nor the time.

But then, he takes my hand and squeezes it, just leaving it there on his thigh. He doesn't look affected by any of this, probably because it doesn't mean anything to him. Plus, he has a lot more on his mind. But it's sending so many sparks straight to my heart that I can't even feel my hand anymore. I was right. I am a terrible person.

"It's so dumb to get this attached, isn't it?" he asks, surprising me.

I frown. "Of course not. They're your dogs. They're a big part of your life."

He lowers his eyes. "My dogs are my best friends, my family. I just can't imagine them being gone, you know?" His voice constricts. "But I know they won't always be here."

"Hey," I say, rubbing his back again. "Don't go there. Bobby's going to be fine. He has to be."

Zane opens his mouth to answer when Luke barges into the room. We both spring to our feet, and my heart thrums rapidly.

"I took a few tissue samples of the stomach and colon. Kathryn should get to them fast. While I was in surgery, I got the other analysis back, and his blood work shows inflammation, a low level of B12—which means a decreased ability to absorb nutrients—and an imbalance in the normal bacterial populations in the GI tract. All of which confirm my diagnosis of IBD. We'll be one hundred percent sure once we have the biopsy results."

Zane seems to hold his breath. "So, he's going to be okay?"

"I think so," Luke says with a smile. "While there is no cure for IBD, we can try different diets, B12 supplementation, and probiotics. I've already started him on an IV to help him feel better."

"Thank you," Zane says, releasing a loud breath. "Do we need to take any precautions?"

Luke once again glances between Zane and me. Yup, I also caught that "we," but he probably meant Seth.

"Nothing in particular. Keeping him inside and isolated would do more harm than good. I would just keep an extra close eye on him and avoid taking him on sled rides for a bit. The vomiting made him a little weak. Oh, and no treats."

Zane nods rapidly. "Okay. Thank you, Luke."

They shake hands, and Luke slaps Zane's back. "He'll be fine. We'll figure out something that works for the big guy, and he'll be back to normal in no time."

"Can we see him?" I ask, dying to pet my furry friend.

Luke grins. "Of course. He's still a little drowsy from the anesthesia, so don't worry if he doesn't move too much."

Zane nods and takes my hand as we walk to the recovery room. And I'm reminded, once again, what a terrible person I am as my heart somersaults in my chest.

Zane

A wave of relief floods me as we park the car in the dark yard. Ivy yawns beside me, and I suddenly realize how tired I am myself. It's been a heck of a day. Well, technically *yesterday* was, since it's now three a.m.

Bobby's feeling a little better, but I still carry him out of the car once I open the door, then haul him inside the barn. He gets a warm welcome from the other dogs once

I lay him on a blanket, and I take a look around, making sure there's nothing that could injure him.

Ivy and I pet him a few more times, and he curls up on the blanket, ready to sleep. It's been a long day for everyone.

Sighing, I take one last look at him before we walk out of the barn.

"I'm glad he's okay," Ivy says, rubbing her hands together before pulling her gloves out of her pockets. "I was so scared."

My throat closes up, and a shiver runs through me. "Me too."

"Can I check on him tomorrow?" Her big emerald eyes are still brimming with concern.

There are no words to express the gratitude I feel toward her. For choosing to be here for me today, for Bobby. For caring as much as she does. "Of course you can. You're welcome anytime. Thank you, Ivy. It means a lot that you came with me. I didn't know it at the time, but I'm glad I wasn't alone." Having her beside me in that waiting room was the only thing keeping me sane. I focused on her hand in mine and her soothing words of comfort. As we'd sat there, I'd never felt so close to her. To anyone. Sofia liked the dogs, but she would have never gone to those lengths for any of them.

"Don't even mention it," she murmurs. "I didn't want you to go through this alone." I lean forward to hug her, but she sighs loudly. "Well, I think we'd better call it a night. And we don't have to do our lesson or go on that hiking trip tomorrow. You should stay with your dogs."

I'm tempted to agree, but I want to do something nice for her. To thank her for her kindness. And to spend more time with her before it's too late. "Nonsense. We'll do both. What kind of teacher would I be if I let you skip class?"

She winces. "Well, I'm outside with my teacher at three in the morning, so I think we're past protocol."

I scratch my head and chuckle. "Right. But Daisy and Seth will be here to look after him. Besides, skiing and hiking would take my mind off everything, so you'd really be doing me a favor." And I'm craving more alone time with Ivy, especially since it has an expiration date. The thought makes my stomach twist.

Her eyebrows knit together, and I'm reminded once again how beautiful she looks under every circumstance. "Are you sure?"

"One hundred percent," I say firmly. "It's the least I can do after what you did for me and Bobby today. Last thing I want is to ruin your vacation."

"No. You're not ruining it, Zane. It's the opposite," she says, and suddenly, she feels incredibly close to me. So close, her flowery perfume envelops me as her eyes widen ever so slightly. "You're the only reason this vacation has been fun, or that I'm still here." Her last words die into a whisper as we lock eyes.

I swallow hard, wondering how I can express my gratitude for tonight and let her know how I feel about her. Would she let me kiss her? Because there's nothing I want more right now.

Just when I'm about to make my move, she clears her throat and averts her eyes. Looks like I have my answer.

"Anyway, see you tomorrow." She spins around and starts to walk away.

"Wait," I call out, way too loudly for both the hour of the night and our proximity. "I'll take you back to your hotel."

She turns around and throws me a pretty smile. "You don't have to. Stay with Bobby. Besides, I'm pretty sure there aren't any serial killers in Winter Heights. Not enough variety for them." She winks, and that makes the corners of my mouth twitch into a smile. I had never smiled this much until I met Ivy. I didn't know I'd like it. Crave it.

I shake my head, ambling toward her. "Can't take any chances. I'll walk with you."

We wander toward the hotel in a silence that matches our surroundings. I've always loved Winter Heights at night. Not that it's particularly loud during the day, but there's an extra level of peace and quiet once the hustle and bustle dies down.

"Thanks for walking me back," she says once we reach the front entrance. Her nose is red from the cold, and her cheeks are flushed. The sudden urge to kiss her overwhelms me again, but I keep it locked up, reminding myself that it's clearly not what she wants right now.

"Of course." I give her a gentle nod, placing my hands in my pockets so I don't accidentally take her into my arms and kiss her into oblivion. "Maybe we could meet an hour later than usual tomorrow? Try and catch a few more winks."

She rocks on her heels, biting her lip. "Sounds good."

Gosh, she really has to stop doing that. I swallow what feels like a ton of bricks and give her a single curt nod before turning around and walking away from her. After everything I've endured today, somehow, it feels like the hardest thing I've done.

25

Crave

Ivy

My night of sleep was short but eventful. I kept dreaming of Zane kissing me, no matter how many times I woke up and fell asleep again. That's everyone's wish, right? Going back to the dream you were just in? Mine too. Except when I'm kissing a guy who lives thousands of miles away, has a totally different lifestyle than mine, *and* is probably not even interested in me.

I draw open the curtains to look outside, but I'm not rewarded by the usual white coat of snow glistening under the sparkling sun. A thick fog has settled over Winter Heights, and I can't even see the peak of the mountain anymore.

It seems like the perfect day to stay inside and soak in the bathtub with a book, but I'm seeing Zane today, and nothing beats that. So, I get dressed in extra warm layers and walk to our meeting point.

"Hey," I say when I glimpse him coming. He's wearing a bigger coat than usual, and the gray beanie on his head makes his eyes pop even more. "How's Bobby?"

The corners of his lips twitch into a smile. "What about me, huh? Only have eyes for Bobby."

I shake my head, rolling my eyes.

"He's good. He even wagged his tail when I came in to feed him this morning, so that's a good sign. He's not a huge fan of the new food I'm giving him, but he ate everything."

My heart soars in my chest. "Glad to hear it."

"Are you sure you want to go out there?" he asks, glancing at the mountain. "Conditions aren't ideal."

I nod. "It's just a little fog. Let's go." I want to make the most of my time here, which is soon coming to an end.

But as it turns out, it wasn't just a little fog. The higher we go up the mountain, the thicker it gets, and the less visibility we have.

"Let's just stop here," Zane says after our second descent. "It's not a good day to ski."

He's right. Most of the slopes are empty—or maybe I just can't see people because of the fog. Either way, I'm fine with ending our session now. I'm wet and uncomfortable, and that bath is really starting to sound like heaven.

"Yeah, I'm struggling," I say, leaning on my poles. "Maybe we should cancel our hiking trip? It's a shame, though. I was looking forward to going. I only have two days left."

He scratches his beard. "I know. I really want to go too. We'll see if it clears out this afternoon. Otherwise, we'll postpone it till tomorrow. Come by the farm after lunch, and we'll figure it out."

The prospect of going to Zane's farm again to see the dogs and spend time with him, even if we can't go out, rejuvenates me in an instant.

We say goodbye, and I hustle back to my hotel where I soak in that bathtub and order room service.

The weather is getting worse by the minute, with the wind picking up and snowflakes starting to fall, and it's a struggle to reach Zane's farm. I have no doubt our hiking expedition is now out of the question. The whole farm looks like a giant icicle. Everything is covered in a glimmering layer of ice, and the large barn door that allows the dogs to go out has been shut. When the wind batters my face, I hurry to the main house and knock on the door.

Zane swings the door open, and as always, the sight of him almost takes my breath away. Especially when he's only wearing a thin sweater. "Hey, come in."

He steps aside, letting me in before shutting the door, and I love how his place smells just like him. Fresh Mountain Man Scent. That's how I'd label that candle.

"This weather is crazy," I say, taking off my coat, beanie, and gloves. "It's warm in here."

He arches an eyebrow. "Why the tone of surprise? You thought I lived in an ice castle?"

I glance around. "Something like that."

The entrance opens to a large living area divided in three sections. On the left is a rustic kitchen with dark wood counters and green floor tiles. In the middle, is a dining room with a large wooden table and a vintage-looking china cabinet. On the right, the living room hosts two large dark-blue couches facing a TV. The coffee table sits on a wide rug and is crowded with magazines, a remote, and a scented candle. A fireplace roars on the side of the room, warming the space and casting a soft orange glow on everything it touches. I definitely expected his home to be a lot less welcoming. It's obviously old and hasn't been renovated, but it looks like it's been well-maintained throughout the years, and effort was made on the decor. I even spot a plant in one corner of the dining room as well as a large framed picture of Zane with his brother, sister, Belinda, and who I assume to be Bruce near the entrance of the house. The immediate vibe this place gives me is "cozy vintage farm that's been lived in."

Shaking his head, Zane laughs hard. "Sorry to disappoint, but this weather is too hardcore even for me. Haven't you seen? Even the dogs are inside."

I pout. "Yeah. Poor puppies. Are they scared, all alone in that barn? What about Bobby?"

"There are twenty of them," he jokes. "They're definitely not alone. But I was with them earlier, and we can go spend some time with them if you want. Bobby's still doing good, but I'm sure he'd love to see you."

A large smile tugs at my lips. "Sure. Are we alone? Where are Seth and Daisy?"

"I sent Seth home at lunchtime—we're clearly not working today—and Daisy is at Belinda's this afternoon. So yeah, we're alone. If you don't count the twenty monsters in the barn."

I swallow hard, trying to ignore the burning in my body at the thought of being alone with Zane in this extremely cozy house. "Well then, let's go see them."

I don't know how long we spend playing with the dogs and cuddling them, but I could do this all day. They're so affectionate and incredibly goofy. It's enough entertainment to last a lifetime. They do get a bit of hair on my clothes, but who cares? Bobby earns an entire cuddling session before I let him rest and return to the others. And the biggest bonus—watching Zane playing with the huskies and kissing their furry heads. He lights up around the pooches and uses that cute dog voice to talk to them. You can tell he's not holding back. This is clearly his happy place.

"You're pretty lucky to have them. This way, you're never alone."

"I know it." He chuckles, the sound going straight to my heart. "It's both a curse and a blessing."

"I think I'm going to get a puppy too, or a cat, maybe. They're more independent, and I work long hours. I just can't bear the thought of coming home to an empty house, you know?" I sigh. "I used to live with my sister before she left for France, and after that, Dan moved in. I don't think I'll like living alone."

A slight wrinkle forms on Zane's forehead as he scratches behind Bella's ear—or maybe it's Buffy. I'm not sure. "You don't have any family or friends around?"

I drop my hands to my knees. "Nope. I have some acquaintances, of course, and my work colleagues, but my sister is my best friend. I'm happy for her, but I didn't realize how big of an impact her move to Paris would have on me. Well, I guess the impact shouldn't have been that big since I was supposed to live with my husband. On top of that, most of our friends were his."

The realization that I'm now utterly alone hits hard. How did I not see it before? Without my sister or Dan, I have no one. I lie down on the hay, and Burger comes to sniff my face. "Oh gosh. My life is a mess, and here I am, babbling to you about my problems. This new year is just far from what I thought it would look like."

He leans down next to me, his shoulder grazing mine, and my pulse quickens. "I get it. But sometimes, the most unexpected things in life are the most beautiful." He turns to face me, and we lock eyes. A whirlwind of emotions consumes me. I'm trying to make sense of it when Bella walks over Zane's chest and starts licking him all over the face.

Yup. You and me both, girl. Only I don't have the guts.

After a few more minutes of puppy play time, we head back to Zane's house. We hear the wind picking up as we take off our coats. Walking over to the kitchen window, Zane peers at the driving snow that has started to fall.

"It's getting really bad out there," he says, turning to me. "You should stay here tonight. Even walking the half mile to your hotel could be dangerous. The roads will be icy."

My heart surges in my chest. Spending the night here with Zane? I don't think I could ever agree to that without putting in peril every effort I've made until now to suppress the desire burning inside me every time I lay eyes on him.

But then again, it's for my own safety.

"Right." I bite my bottom lip. "Are you sure? I don't want to impose."

He shakes his head, his Adam's apple bobbing. "You're not. I'll make some dinner, and then we can watch a movie?"

"Who are you?" I strangle out a laugh. "Cooking and a movie? Is that really your thing?"

He tilts his head to the side, clearly amused. "You took me to a cooking lesson, remember? I'm now a certified chef. And I actually don't watch many movies, but I thought it might be something you'd like."

I wipe my palms on my pants. It's getting warmer by the second in here. "Sure. That'd be great."

Zane

Ivy is bustling around my kitchen, helping me make dinner. And the truth is, I *want* her here. I long for her touch as we bump into each other, reaching for the same utensil, or when her body brushes against mine when she passes behind me. I have totally and utterly fallen for Ivy Clark, and I'm not sure what to do about it. All I know is that I can't let her out into a snowstorm, so here we are. I know I said hair removal was the ultimate torture. Well, I take it back. Spending the night indoors with the woman you like when you're well aware the feeling's not mutual? That's the real torture. The worst kind. The kind you hate but also crave deep inside.

We're almost done preparing our fancy meal—spaghetti and meatballs—when Daisy calls to let me know she's staying at Belinda's tonight. She doesn't want to leave her alone in this weather, and I don't argue.

The food is pretty good, though there is a lot of room for improvement. Maybe I should suck it up and book another lesson with Giuseppe. Everyone says the way to a man's heart is through his stomach. Maybe it's the same for women? Luckily, Ivy doesn't complain and eats everything on her plate.

Once we clear the table, we settle on the couch. Ivy is sitting right next to me, the cozy throw blanket covering her. We go for an old classic, *Home Alone*.

It's one of the few movies I've actually seen and enjoy, but I can't concentrate on Kevin's shenanigans with Ivy huddled so close to me. Her perfume, the sound of her laughter, her velvety skin inches from mine. It's just too much. My mind starts spiraling, my heart thundering in my chest, threatening to burst out. I'm on sensory overload.

At this point, I'm not even watching the movie anymore. How can I when the most gorgeous woman on the planet is sitting next to me?

Probably feeling my gaze, she turns to face me, and I see a gleam in her emerald eyes that wasn't there before. It mirrors the way I'm feeling inside, and suddenly, the debate about whether to kiss her vanishes.

Tucking a strand of hair behind her ear, I plunge my gaze into hers, ready to kiss her. But without warning, she leans forward first, pressing her velvety lips on mine in a featherlight kiss. Her touch is soft and tentative, like she's just testing the waters. My world tilts on its axis, heart bouncing in my ribcage. And in this moment, I know it's never going to be enough. Now that I've had a taste, I'm craving more.

Cupping her face with my palm, I urge her closer, and our mouths collapse against each other again. Harder this time. It's like the New Year's fireworks are exploding all over again, except this time, they're in my stomach and booming louder than ever before.

I pull back for a second, studying her, and the raw look in her eyes consumes me. She clutches my shirt, closing the gap between us. Her lips are like liquid fire on mine, igniting a flame I didn't know existed.

We can't stop now. At least, I know I can't. All I want is to keep kissing Ivy over and over again. And I'm the luckiest man in the entire world, because she lets me.

26

Happy

Ivy

I don't do casual or flings or whatever. Now that the sun is up, and I'm half-lying on Zane's couch, everything hits me. *Hard*. I glance to my side, careful not to wake him. He looks so peaceful in his sleep, even in this awkward half-lying position. Last night was amazing, the best I've had in years. And that kiss . . . That kiss and all the others that followed were incredible, but they also change everything, because I now find myself wanting more. Just like I knew I would. Zane's not the type of guy you casually date. He's kind and funny and has so many layers to his personality, a lifetime wouldn't be enough to get to know him. Whenever I see him, all I want to do is call one of my colleagues to pack up my apartment and ship my things here so I can be with him. My heart twists, holding me hostage. Because I know that's not happening. That's not how it works. I'm leaving in two days and will probably never see him again.

Zane stirs next to me and opens his eyes. "Hey beautiful."

Dang it. Why did he have to say that?

He sits up, takes my hand in his, and runs his fingers over my knuckles. His touch sends shivers down my spine. I'm about to reply when he leans forward, capturing my mouth in a sweet kiss. It's a tender kiss, his lips brushing mine softly, as if he's savoring every second.

"I've been wanting to do that again since last night," he says against my lips.

A smile breaks onto my face. "Good morning. Sleep well?"

He stretches his arms. "Very. Do you want some breakfast? I can make eggs and bacon. Even toast, assuming Daisy hasn't eaten all the bread."

"Sounds good," I chirp, even though his casual demeanor is making me freak out even more. Who needs breakfast right now? The two of us have to talk this out. *Stat*.

He whips us up some omelets and bacon, and I just watch, unable to stop ruminating like a complete worry wart.

"Breakfast is served," he says, sliding a plate in front of me on the kitchen table.

I force a smile. "Thanks."

We dig into our food and begin eating in silence, but I just can't take it any longer. I drop my fork on the table. "Listen, I don't kiss random people. Maybe you're looking for a vacation fling, but I'm not. It's not me, and now I'm rambling, and please just say something."

"Neither am I," he responds with a small smile.

A loud breath eases out of my lungs, but I'm still tense. "Really? But I thought—the other day you said you didn't want to date after what happened with your ex."

He cocks his head to the side, and I notice a glint of vulnerability in his gray eyes. "You said the same."

I bite my lip. "I know. I guess things can change. But still, I live thousands of miles away, Zane, and I leave in two days. Any kind of relationship would be doomed from the start."

"Can we just be happy for a minute?" he asks with a lopsided smile. "Cause, you know, I haven't had that in a while."

I want to argue, push for us to figure this out, but I haven't been happy in a while either. And honestly, that sounds like heaven right now. I guess we can be happy now and freak out later. Procrastination at its finest.

I nod in agreement, and he leans over the table to place another sweet kiss on my lips. Happy it is.

After we both take a shower, Zane grabs a change of clothes for me from Daisy's room. I feel a little weird about borrowing her stuff, but Zane assures me she won't mind. I've been wearing the same clothes since yesterday afternoon, so he doesn't have much convincing to do.

"So, what should we do today? Snowshoeing?" he asks.

A surge of excitement courses through me. "I'd love to. If the weather permits?"

He walks to the window and looks outside. "The sky is clear, and it's always fun to hike after a storm. Lots of fresh powder on the ground. It's more physical, though, so it's up to you."

I slap a hand on the table, ready to tackle the day. "Let's do it."

"Great. I just have to check on the dogs first and make sure either Seth or Daisy is here before we go."

I pull my brown hair into a ponytail. "Of course. Let's go."

The dogs jump for joy as soon as we push the barn doors open. After a few cuddles—Bobby getting a little extra—Zane opens their back door, and they rush outside to play in the snow. I'm really going to miss these pups when I go. I can almost name them all now. I shake the thought away, chiding myself. Today, we're enjoying ourselves. *Happy.*

We proceed to feed them, and we're just finishing cleaning their pen when Seth enters the barn.

"Good morning." Seth's eyes fall on me, and from the way his eyebrows twitch, he's obviously surprised. But he doesn't say anything.

"Hey, how are you?" Zane asks, shoveling another scoop of dog poop into a bucket. "Did the storm do any damage?"

Seth shakes his head. "Everything seems okay. I saw a tree down, but that's it. Even Mathilda is still up."

"Who's Mathilda?" I ask.

"The town statue," Zane says, dusting off his hands. "She always topples over during big storms. We keep patching her up and propping her back on her feet. That gal is tough. Still hanging in there after all these storms."

"Exactly. So it couldn't have been that big of a storm," Seth says before turning to Zane. "Are you here today? Will you lead the rides?"

"Nope. Today, I'm enjoying myself." Zane winks at him before walking over to me. "You're on. Ivy and I are going hiking." He takes my hand to bring me closer, then kisses me. It's a chaste kiss at first, but then, his finger grazes my cheek, and we're both hungry for more. I feel bad for poor Seth, just standing there, but I can't pass up one of Zane's kisses. Ever.

A loud whistle cracks the silence, followed by a dog barking. "Well, well. About time."

"Daisy," Zane says, breaking away. "Was everything all right at Belinda's last night?"

"Of course. Just like here, apparently." She waggles her eyebrows. "I love your outfit, Ivy."

My cheeks catch fire. "I—Not what you're thinking. I just had the same clothes on since yesterday. I'm sorry. Zane said it would be okay."

She laughs, and the pretty sound fills the barn. "It's fine. You can borrow clothes from me anytime if you put such a big smile on my brother's face."

Zane rakes a hand through his light-brown hair. "So, Ivy and I are going on a hike."

"Are you taking a dog or two?" Seth asks. "I could prep them."

Zane glances at me, raising his eyebrows in question.

"Oh yes, please," I squeal, jumping in place. "I didn't know they could come."

Zane scoffs. "Are you kidding? They'd love to tag along."

"Can we take Bella and Burger?"

He arches an eyebrow. "Already have your favorites, huh?"

"Of course not," I say, crossing my arms over my chest defensively. "I love them all."

Everyone breaks into laughter.

"I'll prep them," Seth says with a grin.

Zane places his arm around my shoulders. "Let's go make some sandwiches to take with us, and then we can go."

Zane

This is how I love the mountain best. Mounds of fresh powder, clear sky, the cool, crisp air, my dogs and my girl by my side. Some people dream of winning the lottery or traveling the world. *This* is my dream.

The hike gets a little tricky sometimes, even for Bella and Burger, because of the amount of snow that fell last night. But they're loving it. They're covered from paws to neck in snow and seem happier than ever.

Ivy's stunning smile doesn't leave her face, and at this point, the two of us are probably competing for the biggest grin. I'm glad this moment is ours to enjoy. I don't know how we're going to sort this all out, but at least we'll have today to look back on. One happy memory.

As we're passing the edge of the woods, I shake a large pine tree, bringing cascades of snow tumbling onto Ivy like a mini avalanche.

Gasping, she breaks into a laugh, and the dogs start scampering underneath, ecstatic to see some snow falling—as if the entire ground wasn't covered in it already.

Then, out of the blue, Ivy ducks down and pops back up, lobbing a snowball at my chest from the layer of sticky snow that the sun has slightly melted.

"Hey!" I scream, offended by the assault.

With a giggle, she hurries to take cover behind a tree, Bella scampering after her.

"Oh, I see how it is," I call out. "Girls against boys, huh?" Burger stays put next to me.

"Looks like it," Ivy says through a chuckle. Then, she hits me in the chest again. This woman means business.

I retaliate, but she ducks behind a tree, and I miss. Balling some snow, I carefully approach the line of trees, only to get hit again. This time, straight in the face.

"Oh, you are not getting away this time," I yell, and Burger barks next to me. I glimpse her pink beanie poking out, so I take a few steps sideways, and once she's in my line of sight, I throw my ammunition.

The blow lands right on her shoulder, and she lets out a small scream, falling to her knees. "Ouch."

Crap. I hurry to her side, Burger scurrying after me. "Sorry," I say, unable to hide the worry in my voice. "I didn't realize I tossed it that hard. I'm—"

A cold snowball lands straight on my face. I wipe the wet snow off to see Ivy's eyes gleaming with mischief. She stands up, probably about to make a run for it.

"You!" I say, tackling her from behind. "You play dirty."

We roll in the snow, and her giggles mingle with Burger's and Bella's barking. We roll to a stop under a tree.

"What are you going to do now?" she asks, that gorgeous gleam still lighting up her green eyes.

I settle both hands on the snow on each side of her head, then kiss her. She wraps her arms around my neck, and despite being entirely covered in snow, it's suddenly feeling extremely warm out here.

All that walking and fighting worked up our appetite. We feed Bella and Burger first, then sit down to eat our sandwiches while they rest.

"So, Seth seems nice," Ivy says, lying back in the snow.

I do the same, enjoying the warmth of the sun on my face. "He's a good kid. Focused, passionate. He reminds me a lot of myself when I was his age, actually. Bruce took me under his wing, and thanks to him, I actually became someone."

"That's what you want to do with Seth? Mentor him?"

I squeeze some snow in my fist, then release it. "Yeah. His family doesn't have a lot of resources. So, I help him out as much as I can."

She turns her face toward me, her eyes a lighter shade than usual with all the snow reflecting the sunlight. "You're a good man, Zane Harden."

I chuckle lightly. "Have you ever doubted that?"

She taps a finger on her lips in thought.

Taking my sunglasses off, I arch an eyebrow.

She laughs. "I'm kidding. Well, maybe at the very beginning, I thought you were just a grumpy mountain man—"

I arch my eyebrow higher. "Grumpy mountain man?"

"Yeah," she says, giggling. "A little rough around the edges and lacking patience. *But,* as soon as I saw you at your farm, I knew how amazing you were. The way you care for your dogs . . . Only a good man is capable of that. Bruce raised you well."

I recline back in the snow, scratching my beard. "He really did. But who knew having dogs was so appealing to women?"

"You really should watch more movies." She laughs.

"Why would I want to watch fiction when reality looks like this?" I spread my arms out to gesture widely. "I'm literally in my backyard."

"Yeah." She lets out a satisfied sigh. "It's pretty darn great."

"So are you," I say, looking at her. "Being here with you, on this mountain, is all I'll ever need."

She rolls into my arms. Lifting her chin, I place a soft kiss on her velvety lips.

Perfect. This is perfection.

I don't know how long we stay there lying in the snow, enjoying each other's company and the pure mountain air.

After a while, we continue our walk before turning around to meander back home. It's as pleasant as the walk over, and the dogs even get to run since we already cleared out the path.

When we're back, we let them join the others, but as we're stepping out of the barn, there's someone standing in the yard. The sight makes my skin prickle.

My jaw drops as I finally find my voice. "Sofia? What are you doing here?"

27

Second Choice

Ivy

Wait. Did he just say *Sofia*? As in, the-girl-who-broke-his-heart Sofia?

Standing in Zane's yard is a tall brunette with a pretty red coat that matches her scarlet lips. Her large brown eyes are brimming with emotion. "Sorry for just showing up," she says, biting her bottom lip in a sexy way I instantly hate. "I just missed you so much. I think we made a mistake, ending things."

He doesn't answer, probably too stunned to process her words. He just looks at her, and I despise everything I see in his eyes. A mix of shock, pain, anger. *Longing?* He was about to ask her to marry him, after all. She wasn't just some casual girlfriend. Of course he still has feelings for her.

"No," Zane says through gritted teeth, his eyes tainted by pain. "*You* made a mistake. *You* left me, remember?" His arms fall to his sides in a swoosh.

She closes her eyes for a second. "I know, and I regret it. I love you, Zane. I never stopped loving you. Maybe we can fix it?"

He shakes his head. "I—no. I've moved on," he says, shifting his gaze to me.

Sofia seems to only just now realize that I'm here. I give her a weak smile. Looks like *Happy* is over now. Awkward is the new star of the show.

She covers her face with her hands, then shakes her head. "Oh, gosh. I am so sorry. I didn't—of course you have. You know what, I should just go," she says before hurrying away.

"No," I blurt out. "I should go." My heart constricts as the words leave my mouth, but I know it's the right thing to do.

"What?" Zane turns to me, a mixed expression of pain and surprise contorting his face. "Ivy," he whispers, coming closer. "There's nothing between Sofia and me."

I press my lips together, swallowing hard. "You two should at least talk and figure this out."

He shakes his head vigorously. "There is nothing to figure out."

"Of course there is." I let out a sigh. "You were in love, she broke your heart, and now she's back."

"It doesn't matter. It's too late for that," he says, grabbing my hand. "Ivy, why are you crying?"

I didn't even realize that tears were rolling down my cheeks. My skin must be so used to feeling them by now, I don't even notice them anymore. I dry them with the back of my hand, then flash him a big smile. "I'm fine. What we had was great, but it wasn't meant to last, Zane. We always knew that. We had our happy day, but we can't change the fact that I have to leave. Wanting it to be different won't change anything. Don't risk your chance at real love for some vacation fling."

My entire body aches, and I feel like the oxygen has been sucked from my lungs. But I had to say it. I saw that look. The look that says it might not be totally over for them. The same one I would have seen in Dan's eyes if we'd run into his ex while we were together.

Zane's gaze falls.

"You and I have no future together," I continue, because apparently, I'm a masochist like that. "We have totally different lives. We live in different states. We're not going to make it, but you and Sofia might have a shot. She's back, and if you can forgive her, you'll be happy again." I drop my hand.

"Ivy . . ."

"Thanks for giving me the best vacation ever." I hug him one last time, mentally bottling his pine scent and relegating it to memory.

As I walk away, I feel like I have ski boots on. Each step hurts more than the next. I hate that it ended like this, but somehow, I knew in my heart that it would. How could this ever be more than a fling? I'll never give my heart to a man who's not yet over his ex. Been there, done that. And I really don't recommend it.

When I finally reach my hotel, my face is drenched with tears. Why does this always happen to me? Why am I always someone's second choice? Why can't things ever go my way?

As soon as I drag myself to my room, I open the airline app. I think it's time for me to go home.

Zane

I want to call after Ivy, scream even. But I let her go, because I know that deep down, she's right. I just wanted to live this fantasy a little longer. Happy was good while it lasted. Now, it's just sadness and emptiness.

"Why are you here?" I ask Sofia, who's still standing in the middle of the yard.

"Like I said." She takes a shy step forward. "I missed you. Leaving was a mistake, I realize that now. I know what we had was real."

My heart pinches in my chest. "You left me after spending a year together. You *left*, Sofia…" *Just when I was about to propose,* I'm tempted to add.

"Well, I regret it. It was so dumb to leave you just because I wanted to live somewhere else. It doesn't matter where you live. It's the people around you that make your life a happy one. I'd like to give us a chance. I could move back here, and we can—"

"It's too late," I snap. Which is the truth. If she'd come back a few weeks ago, I would have probably given her that second chance, but things are different now. Everything changed. Even if Ivy doesn't want to be with me, it doesn't change the fact that I no longer want to be with Sofia. If there's one thing being with Ivy made me realize, it's how easy dating the right person can be. No feeling like she's not enjoying herself or listening to her always comparing the small town with the big city. Sofia and I didn't really have much in common.

Her eyes water. "It doesn't have to be too late. We can make this work. I know we can."

"No, we can't, Sofia," I say, spinning on my heel.

"Please, let me explain, apologize... We can figure things out."

I whip back around. "There is nothing to figure out. I'm sorry, but I don't love you anymore. Please go."

That's when it hits me. I'm in love with Ivy. What we had wasn't just a fling, like she suggested. The way we connected was deeper. My feelings *are* deeper. But it turns out, it wasn't the same for her. There wasn't an ounce of hesitation when she decided to leave, or when she claimed I had a shot at happiness with Sofia. Which I don't. Looks like I don't deserve the *happy* thing.

Overwhelmed by my emotions, I drag my feet inside the barn, not bothering to cast one last look at Sofia.

I work the rest of the day, trying to take my mind off Ivy, but it doesn't work. It's as if her face, her smile, her laugh are etched into my brain with permanent ink.

"Hey," Daisy says as she enters the barn, the loud creaking of the door following her.

I mumble a response. The last thing I need is my sister getting on my nerves right now.

"So, that was tense earlier." She lets out a nervous chuckle.

I stop shoveling hay. "You saw that?"

Her face twists into a grimace. "I did, but I wanted to give you some time to cool off. Are you okay now?"

"Still not cooled off." I return to the task at hand.

"For what it's worth, I think Ivy's full of crap." She glances at the ground. "No pun intended."

My lips twitch, but it's not quite a smile.

"She's totally into you, just like you're into her." Daisy's words burn through my chest to my heart, and I want to bask in them as much as I want to shovel them away.

"Nope. You didn't read her right," I say, shoveling harder than necessary, grime splashing my pants.

"Of course I did. I saw the way she looked at you—at the New Year's Eve party and this morning. This was not just a fling for her, Zane. I can guarantee you that much."

I snicker. "What? Are you a mind reader now?"

She gives me a pointed look. "We girls, we know things. We're able to see beneath the surface, and I'm telling you, this was more."

I groan. "You know, it'd be nice if you could share that magic decoder of yours."

She taps her chest. "Girls' honor. We can't. But you have to talk to her. Just tell her how you feel, and she'll open up."

I stop shoveling, staring down at the floor. "Are you sure about that?"

"Positive. Besides, what do you have to lose? Just give her time to breathe, and talk to her tomorrow. It's her last day, right?"

I scratch my head. "Yeah. She's leaving the day after tomorrow. We have our last lesson at ten."

"There you go."

I let out a small breath. Guess I'll just rack my brain all day and night to decide how I'm going to tell her that we have to give us a shot. "Thanks, Daisy."

She gives a dramatic bow. "At your service."

"What about you? How long until you fly back to Chicago?"

"Ready to kick me out, are you?" She pouts. "And after I just gave you such amazing advice? No loyalty."

I roll my eyes. "Oh, come on. I'm not kicking you out. You've always been such a drama queen. It's just a question, since we're talking about relationships and all that."

She shrugs, twirling the ends of her hair around a finger. "I don't miss Todd anymore, and I know I'm doing the right thing. I'll just move in with Lucy. Hopefully, the city is big enough that we won't have to cross paths ever again."

"I'm proud of you for looking after yourself and making that decision. It's not easy." My heart gains another crack at the thought of my little sister suffering through all that heartache, most of it alone. I wish I could barricade her in Winter Heights so I can protect her, but just like I hate to be cooped up inside, Daisy is made for city life.

"It was pretty tough, but I reached a point where it was either that or my sanity, so . . ."

"You really have grown up. Who knew?" I try to give her a side hug, but she pushes me away.

"Ew. No, you're all splashed in dog poo."

I shake my head. "Just when I was about to say I might actually miss you."

She sticks out her tongue just like she used to when she was twelve. "You'll totally miss me."

"Nope," I say, going back to shoveling.

"Yeah you will."

I roll my eyes. "Okay, maybe a little."

"Good. Because I'll miss you lots." Wrapping her arms around my waist, she hugs me tight.

"What about dog—"

"Shh. You're ruining the moment. Just enjoy it."

And I do, because I really need a hug right now. Even if she did give me hope with Ivy, that was way too many emotions in such a short period of time. And, *okay.* Also because I love my little sister, and I'm really going to miss her when she leaves.

I barely slept last night, but I'm not tired. I've rehearsed over a million times what I'll say to Ivy when I see her. In the end, I decide to just be blunt and ask her where she stands. I've always been a straight shooter, and if there was ever a time for that approach to make sense, it's now. At least that way, there is no room for double meanings, and we can figure things out from there. *If* there is anything to figure out.

As much as I would love Daisy to be right, I don't trust her love sensor—or whatever she calls it—one hundred percent. There's always a margin for error. Meaning there's still the possibility that Ivy doesn't want this. That it was just a little rebound fling after her failed almost-marriage. After all, she was quick to leave me in the hands of Sofia yesterday. No, let's not go there. *Happy thoughts.*

I stop at the shack to grab the equipment and print out her end-of-the-week diploma. It doesn't mean anything, of course. It's just something Darwin likes to give his clients after their lessons. A little souvenir to bring home with them.

I put it into a sleeve, tuck it in my coat, and walk to the meeting point, my anxiety building by the minute. It's a beautiful morning, and I'm glad we'll at least have one last fun day together. I think she might even be ready to go to the highest point on the mountain.

From where I'm standing, I can see her hotel's front entrance, and every time the sliding doors open, my heart leaps. But once again, it's not Ivy. *It's never Ivy.* The hope of seeing her emerge from the hotel diminishes with every minute I wait, until it's completely crushed.

Picking up the equipment, I march toward the hotel, determination burning inside me. She can't just ghost me like that. I'm her teacher, after all. Plus, I have this very important diploma to give to her. *And* we need to talk. Maybe it was dumb of me to assume she'd show up for the lesson. Maybe she already said her goodbyes yesterday. Well, I didn't.

"Hi," I say to the receptionist when I reach the lobby. "Would you mind calling room 528 for me, please? Ivy Clark."

"Of course." She picks up her phone, types something on her keyboard, then frowns. "I'm sorry, but Ms. Clark left this morning."

"Oh, that's fine. I'll just wait here, or maybe I'll find her in town. It's not that big."

I'll go into every store on this street or wait in front of the hotel all day if I have to.

The receptionist shakes her head. "No, I mean Ms. Clark checked out. Are you Mr. Harden? She left some clothes for you."

And just like that, it's like I've been hit in the chest by a snow shovel. "She's gone?" I breathe out.

"I'm afraid so." She takes a box from the shelf labeled "laundry" and hands it to me. "There you go. She had it cleaned for you."

I mumble a thank you, grabbing Daisy's clothes and fleeing the lobby. Ivy's gone. She just *left*. Didn't even say goodbye. Why do the women in my life just up and leave me? Am I not enough for them? My entire world darkens, and I'm having a hard time breathing as I exit the building. Outside, everyone is happy and bright, and I suddenly wish an avalanche would just cover them all so I could be alone.

Daisy was wrong. As it turns out, Ivy didn't want anything more to do with me. She came here to heal her broken heart, but instead, she just passed it on to me.

28

The People Around You

Ivy

I'm home. I managed to catch an earlier flight, and even if it took me three planes and a car ride to get here—and the journey set me back a hefty sum—I'm finally home. But the heartache and sorrow doesn't vanish with the snow. It only intensifies as I lay eyes on the wedding gifts still piled in my living room. And every time Zane's face appears in front of my eyes, I break down in tears. Looks like I'm right back to square one.

I need to get rid of all of this. I left home with a broken heart, and now I'm returning with a shattered one. It's even worse now because Zane healed each and every one of my wounds, but the bandages didn't stick, and now my heart is ruined beyond repair.

But I made the right decision. I *had* to leave. I won't be someone's second choice ever again. Plus, there's the whole we-don't-even-live-in-the-same-state thing. Sometimes, you have to see things for what they are. When the obstacles are too tall to surmount, maybe they're not meant to be overcome.

After cleaning the mess in my living room and stacking all the gifts near the entrance, I collapse on the couch and call Hazel to tell her everything that happened.

"Well, damn," she mumbles into the receiver, clearly stunned. "I kept hoping you'd follow your big sister's footsteps and find yourself a perfect man on your vacation, but . . ."

I furrow my eyebrows. "Really? But you told me to have a fling."

"Yeah, knowing full well that isn't your style," she says, as if it should have been obvious. "I thought you'd be so smitten that you'd end up moving thousands of miles away to be with him."

My heart twists painfully. "So did I." The thought of moving to Winter Heights crossed my mind more than once this past week, especially that night after we kissed. I could see myself living there. I could have been happy there, I know it. Nurses are always in high demand everywhere, and there's something about the town that went straight to my heart. But his number one choice came back.

"Wait, really?" I can practically hear Hazel's frown through the phone. "I was just joking."

I blow out a breath. "I thought it was fate, you know? That I'd been sent to Winter Heights for a reason. That *all* of this happened for a reason. Dan leaving me before the wedding, me going on my honeymoon alone, Zane having to step up for his brother. It felt like it was meant to be. Serendipity. But now, I'm sure there's no such thing as fate. And the truth is, I'm just not good enough to be someone's first choice."

"Ivy," she says in a scolding tone. "Don't say that, please. Of course you are." Her voice softens. "You're amazing. Just because it didn't work out this time doesn't mean it never will."

I swallow the lump in my throat, forcing her words to sink in, but I don't think that will ever feel true for me. Not when it happens twice within the span of two weeks.

Some people are just not meant to have a happy ending. And maybe I'm one of them.

Zane

Over the next few days, I mostly stay inside, which quickly leads to a flow of visitors at my bedroom door. Exactly what I need.

First up is Daisy, who still thinks she's right and keeps telling me to call Ivy. I shut the door in her face, telling her to leave me alone. She eventually does and flies back to Chicago. I do hug my little sister before she leaves, and she manages to speak to me for a whole five minutes without mentioning my misery.

Then, my brother stops by, first with Aaron and then by himself, telling me to man up and stop sulking. That if I want something, I just have to go after it. Easy for him to say when he already has everything he could ever want.

Finally, there's Belinda, who brings me food twice a day. But at least she has the presence of mind not to twist the knife in my wounds. She really just wants to make sure I'm eating and basically, that I'm still alive.

Someone knocks on my door again, and I'm betting on Darwin this time. Belinda already stopped in a few hours ago with lunch.

Grunting, I haul myself off the couch in my bedroom and open the door. As soon as I do, Boomer woofs and scampers into the room with more energy than he's displayed in weeks.

"Hey, boy," I say, scratching his jaws. He licks my face before trying to jump in place, but his old age keeps him grounded.

"He missed you," Belinda says with a faint smile. "I thought some animal company might do you good. Seth says you've only gone down to the barn twice these past few days.

Can she blame me? Everything reminds me of Ivy. The barn, the dogs, the whole main floor of the house.

"Thanks," I say, kneeling down to keep petting Boomer, who's now lying on my carpet.

Belinda sits down on the armchair by the window but doesn't say anything. I keep my attention focused on Boomer.

"I'm worried about you," she finally says. I knew it was too good to be true. "I've never seen you like this, Zane."

Zane? When was the last time she called me Zane? She never calls me by my first name. Except to scold me when I was young, or in especially serious situations.

I want to form a coherent sentence, but my throat constricts. This *is* serious. Ivy completely broke me. How could she hold so much power over me when I just met her days ago?

"I told you to be careful when she first came into town, but I really wanted to be wrong. Especially when I saw you two at the party. She seemed different, and the two of you together seemed *right*. I wish I could have been off the mark, my boy. I'm sorry I wasn't. But you have to get over this. Though heartbreaks are hard, they do heal eventually. You have so much to be thankful for. You just have to get past this."

I grunt, but it almost sounds like a moan. "It's all Sofia's fault."

Frowning, she tilts her head to the side. "Your ex, Sofia? What does she have to do with this?"

It's my turn to grimace. "Didn't Daisy or Darwin tell you? I was with Ivy in the yard when Sofia showed up, asking me to give her a second chance."

Her eyes widen like two saucepans. "What? Why doesn't anyone tell me what's going on around here? I may be old, but I'd still like to be kept in the loop. What did you tell her?"

I shrug. "I thought you knew about that. I made it clear I wasn't interested, but Ivy said I should give her a chance, that what I had with Sofia was worth salvaging while our own relationship was doomed from the start."

"Oh, I see."

I take a deep breath. "If only Sofia hadn't come back, maybe Ivy and I would have had a chance to talk about our future, or at least, she wouldn't have found a reason to reconsider us. And Sofia's arrival probably brought back bad memories from her failed engag—"

And just like that, everything is a lot clearer. What if that's why Ivy left? Because she didn't want to relive that situation? As if I would ever hurt her. She probably thought I was still into Sofia all this time, and my ex showing up only reminded her of how her engagement ended. My heart beats faster with each passing second as it all falls into place. That has to be it. I jump to my feet, startling Boomer who'd just fallen asleep.

"You're scaring me, my boy."

I pat Boomer's head, and he lays it back down on the carpet. "I think I've figured something out. Maybe she loves me too. Maybe she was just scared. I need to talk to her."

"Okay. Just calm down for a second. Take a breath."

"I don't need to calm down." I know why Belinda is saying that. Because if Ivy rejects me again, it'll be worse. But it can't get any worse. I'm barely alive as it is. Finally, I announce, "I'm going to Florida."

She stumbles off her seat. "You are?"

"I have to give this a chance. I'll never breathe again if I don't at least have the final word. Tell Seth he's in charge until I get back."

She tries to talk to me, but I don't listen. Barreling down the stairs, I grab my keys from the coffee table and hop into my truck.

I know this plan is crazy, and Ivy might not want anything to do with me. We've only known each other for ten days, which is seemingly nothing. But in reality, it's *everything* because I've never felt this way before. Being with Ivy is so easy, especially compared to Sofia. I don't have to oversell nature or my dogs to her—she loves it already. She fit in my world so perfectly the second she entered it. That has to count for something, right?

Maybe I'm not enough for her to pack up her life and move here, but she's enough for me to move out and try this big, hot, humid city thing.

Sofia was right about one thing: *It doesn't matter where you live. It's the people around you that make you happy.* I love this place, I truly do. Who wouldn't? Fresh mountain air, real seasons, family surrounding me, being able to work in a career I'm passionate about. But is that enough anymore? I've been miserable since Ivy left. I'm not even living anymore. I've reverted back to being the grump she loved to hate when we first met, and I've stayed shut up inside my room. Even if there's a risk of getting hurt again, I need to know. I have to talk to her face to face and show her that she's the only one I want. I need to tell her that I love her, that we can have it all.

29

Home

Ivy

Can heartbreak dull your senses? Because nothing tastes the same since I've come home. All my senses were heightened in Winter Heights, and here, everything is bland.

I've been dragging myself to work like a zombie these past few days, and I'm glad that my colleagues are tiptoeing around me, acting like I'm a ticking time bomb. That way, I don't have to talk to them. I'm turning into Zane, and the weird thing is, I kind of like it.

On top of losing my senses, I think I'm also in need of a mental checkup.

Today is my day off, and I'm content to spend it on my couch with a carton of ice cream, watching yet another romcom. I wish I could be as brave as the heroines on my TV screen. They go after what they want, even if it means they'll get their heart broken.

The truth is, I've been debating going back to Winter Heights and telling Zane I love him, that I could move there so we could give our relationship a try. But I'm just not strong enough. Besides, I don't think I could recover from a third heartbreak if I get there only to find him with Sofia.

He was still nursing his breakup when I met him. Of course he took her back. Why wouldn't he? Because of a girl he met ten days ago?

I dig my spoon into the vanilla-pecan ice cream and close my eyes as it melts on my tongue. But the usual crackling of my taste buds doesn't come. It never does anymore.

With a sigh, I try to focus on the movie again. The hero is getting ready to perform the grand gesture to get the heroine back.

But because the Universe hates me, someone knocks at my door at the exact same moment. Can't I enjoy anything?

I drag myself to the door, telling myself to be nice to whoever it is even if I want to make them disappear.

But when I swing the door open, it feels as if all the blood drains from my body. I take a step back, widening my eyes further to make sure I'm seeing this right. Zane Harden. On my front porch.

"Ivy," he breathes out, and I have to blink twice to make sure I'm not having some kind of hallucination. He takes my hand, and a tingle courses through me, confirming that he's really here. I'm pretty sure I wouldn't feel that spark of electricity if it wasn't real.

"I'm so happy I found you," he says. "I'm sorry about everything. About Sofia. I should have gone after you right away. I came the next day, and you were already gone. But Ivy, I love you. I want you like I've never wanted anyone in my life. I promise you, there is nothing between Sofia and me anymore. From the moment I met you, you were the only girl I could think about."

I suck in a breath, trying to make sense of everything he's saying.

"We haven't known each other for long, and it's weird that I just jumped on a plane for the first time ever to come here, but there's something between us, Ivy. It was more than just a vacation fling or a rebound."

He wipes the back of his hand on his cheek, and I realize he's sweating. Like, a lot. How is it possible that even sweat looks sexy on him?

My eyes trail down his body, and I notice he's majorly overdressed for the weather. He's wearing a flannel shirt that looks way too thick for the Florida heat, a thick pair of jeans, and the same boots he wore in Winter Heights when we went wine tasting.

"I—you're not with Sofia?" I stammer, unable to form something more coherent.

He squeezes my hand. "No. Going back to Sofia never even crossed my mind. I haven't thought of her in that way since the moment I met you."

My heart leaps, and I have to blink again to make sure I'm not dreaming.

"If you feel the same," he says, swallowing hard before gazing at me with those intense gray eyes, "if you'll have me, I'll move here, and we can give our relationship a try."

My chest tightens. "What? But what about the farm?"

"Seth can take over," he says simply. "He's a fast learner, and the transition won't take too long."

I bite my lip, my mind reeling. He's ready to give up his farm, his dogs, his house, just for me? The thought makes me dizzy, and I lean on the door for support. Maybe I was wrong about being second choice. For once, I'm not just the consolation prize. I'm the real deal. And if Zane is ready to take such a giant leap, I can take a small one. Me moving to Colorado makes way more sense. It's not like I have anything holding me back here. But knowing that Zane would give it all up for me sends shivers through my entire body.

"Or I could come?" I suggest, tilting my head.

He frowns. "What do you mean?"

"I could come back to Winter Heights with you. I have nothing here, and you have everything there. I don't want you to give up Bruce's legacy for me. Besides, I love the dogs and the town. I'll be happy there."

"Ivy," he says, wiping the perspiration from his forehead before pressing it against mine. I smile at the gesture. I would have taken his sweaty brow, but it's so thoughtful of him. Funny how the grump I met ten days ago has turned into the perfect gentleman.

His chest is heaving up and down. "Are you sure?"

"I am, because I feel the same about you."

With a huge grin, he pulls me into a tight embrace. Like he's making sure I'll never leave again. As if I wanted to. Our lips touch, and with every brush of his lips against mine, he tells me how much he wants me. That I'm his first and only choice.

He breaks our kiss, caressing my cheek and looking into my eyes.

"Are you sure you want to move in with me?" he exhales. "Because my offer still stands."

"One hundred percent," I say, leaning into his hand. "Everything that happened between us, and the circumstances that led me to Winter Heights, it's all fate. I'm sure of it. We found each other there, and it was the best time of my life. I don't want that to end. Plus, what's a Siberian husky like you going to do here in sunny Florida?" I joke.

"I'd turn into a summer dog if I needed to." He chuckles, taking my hands in his to bring me closer before placing a soft kiss on my forehead.

I intertwine our fingers. "No need. I just have to find myself a job, but in the meantime, I can help around the farm. Maybe you can even turn me into a musher." I say, waggling my eyebrows. I would actually enjoy that a lot.

"Or you could still be a nurse?" he says, cocking his head. "You saw how slammed Claire was at the clinic. There used to be two, but Anita retired last summer, and Claire needs the extra pair of hands. I know the mayor's been trying to fill that position for months, but applicants don't come easy in Winter Heights."

The moment he suggests it, I can immediately picture myself working there with Claire, coming home to dinner with Zane, helping with the dogs around the farm—and, of course, sneaking tons of puppy cuddles. Maybe there really is something about us Clark sisters only meeting our matches on vacation and moving away to start a new life. Maybe I'll have my happy ending after all. This is all so new, but the way Zane is looking at me right now holds a promise of forever, just like my heart pounding in my chest. "That would be perfect."

"It will be perfect either way," he says, placing a sweet kiss on my lips. "Because you're coming home with me."

Epilogue

Ivy

I've never been happier than during these last sixteen months. Ever since I came to Winter Heights and moved in with the man I love. I got the job at the clinic, and Claire and I make a great team. On the side, I also work with Zane and Seth at the farm.

As I'm walking home after my morning shift at the clinic, admiring the view of the distant mountains, the giddy feeling doesn't dampen. This is my backyard now. And it's magnificent.

As soon as I enter the farm, I zoom to the barn. It's always my first stop when I get home. When you have twenty happy pups waiting for you, there's no other option. Plus, Zane is usually there too.

Today, there is no human life when I reach the barn. But I do get the warmest welcome, as always. The dogs all jump and bark, asking for my attention. I can name them all now, and I immediately notice the ones who are missing—probably on a ride with Seth.

I'm in the middle of a cuddle session with Bobby and Buffy when the door of the barn creaks, and more barking and jumping follow.

"There you are," Zane says, his deep voice rumbling. As always, his booming timbre sends tingles down my spine. Just because it's part of my routine now doesn't mean I've gotten used to it. I'm pretty sure it's impossible to acclimate to Zane's towering presence and gravelly voice. And his scent, his fresh mountain scent. I thought I'd catch it too, now that I live here, but I quickly realize it's not about the location. It's all Zane.

I stand up, and he quickly draws me in, kissing my forehead, cheeks, nose, and then finishing with the sweetest kiss on my lips.

"How was your morning?" he asks, hands settling on my waist.

"Good. Normal day. Not too busy, not too slow. How about you? Did you lead a ride this morning?"

"I did. Took the first one. Seth should be back soon," he says, glancing at his watch. "And he has one more this afternoon. Oh, I was just on the phone with Daisy. She says hi."

"How is she?"

He steps back, rolling his eyes. "Frantic. I could barely understand a word she said. Apparently, she has to convince a New York researcher to join their ranks? But I didn't understand much after that. She started talking about architecture arguments and New York vs Chicago, and she kind of lost me. So, to answer your question, she's . . . alive?"

I chuckle. "Sounds like she has a lot on her plate."

"Yeah. Hey, are we still going on a hike this afternoon?" he asks, wringing his hands.

The town is still getting some snowfall, but it's probably our last month before the off season starts. Not that it's been particularly slow since we started offering hiking and camping trips last summer, and we're already booked solid through late July. But winter is my favorite season in Winter Heights, and once the snow melts, I start to miss hiking through the snow and going on rides with the dogs.

"Of course we are!" I bubble.

Zane's shoulders fall slightly, and if I didn't know him well, I wouldn't have noticed. He goes on plenty of rides and hikes alone, but I know he prefers when I tag along.

I turn to the dogs. "Who wants to go on a hike?"

Zane

I should be reveling in the spectacle Mother Nature is bestowing on us as we trek through the fresh snow, but I can't seem to appreciate the way the sun is sparkling on the thick blanket of white on the ground or the crisp aroma of pine trees. All I can think of is the ring box that's safely tucked in the inside pocket of my coat.

My throat constricts when it hits me. I'm actually doing this. I, Zane Harden, am about to propose to Ivy Clark. And even if I think she's going to say yes, there's that annoying little voice in my head telling me she won't. The same one that prevented me from popping the question in Paris when we attended Olivier and Hazel's wedding in the fall, and on New Year's Day and Valentine's Day. The voice whispers that she got hurt the last time someone proposed to her, and even if she loves me, she won't be able to get past that. We could stay like this, unmarried. We're already living and raising twenty dogs together. It's almost the same thing.

Almost.

Because having Ivy as my wife means eternity. It means her taking my name. It means we're starting a family.

My heart starts racing at the thought. I've never wanted anything this much in my life.

"You're awfully quiet," Ivy says, an eyebrow arching above her sunglasses. The sun is beating down on us, enveloping her in a beautiful glow.

"Just contemplating nature," I say with a smile.

She hooks her arm through mine and sighs. "Yeah. It's so pretty. I'm sad it's already the end of the season."

Blaze and Bandit start barking, chasing each other in the snow, while Boots strolls peacefully next to us. They're going to miss the snow too. I have to make sure they all get their turn this week—either on a ride or a hike.

"Should we take a break here?" Ivy asks as we reach our favorite spot to relax. It's the same place where we had lunch on our first hike together, a peaceful, untouched area at the edge of the forest.

I nod and tell the dogs to stop, but the words get stuck in my throat. This is it.

Ivy and I sit down, and she grabs some snacks out of my bag.

"Sweet or salty?" she asks, waving the bags in front of me.

I shake my head. "Nothing."

Her eyes widen, and she lets out one of her cute chuckles. "Since when do you refuse snacks?"

As if I could eat anything right now. I can barely talk.

She's still looking at me, expecting an answer. That's it. I have to do this now, or I'm going to lose my sanity. Unzipping my coat, I unceremoniously grab the small box and open it.

Ivy gasps, dropping the snacks in the snow.

"Ivy," I say, barely hearing my own voice over the thundering of my heart. "I'm hopelessly in love with you, and I couldn't imagine my life without you. You're the best thing that's ever happened to me. You make me see life in such a different light, a brighter light, and I'm so lucky you saw past my thick shell and grouchy attitude. Now, I want more." I pause, gauging the look on her face. It's giving me shock vibes, but not in a bad way, so I keep going. "I want eternity. Will you marry me?"

She's frozen, unable to utter a word. Her deep green eyes sink into mine, and the silence is deafening.

Finally, Blaze barks loudly, and she clears her throat. "Yes, of course," she gushes with a beaming smile. "Of course I'll marry you."

She falls into my arms, and I hug her so tight I fear I might break her in two.

Yes. She said yes.

My hands cup her face, and I capture her lips in a desperate kiss. She wraps her arms around my neck, drawing me closer until we lose our balance, falling on our sides in the plush snow.

Giggling, she grazes my bottom lip with her teeth, teasing me, before pressing her soft lips to mine. I'll never get tired of Ivy's kisses. They're like candy. The kind of addiction you don't want to overcome.

We part and break for air, but I can't stay away. Brushing my lips against her jaw, I explore every available inch of her, the thrill of shivers on her skin matching the tingles in my chest.

"Thank you for saying yes," I say, placing one more kiss on her sweet lips.

"I love you so much, Zane. There's nothing I want more than to spend the rest of my life with you."

My heart bursts in my chest, and I suddenly feel whole again. For once, I'm completely satisfied. All my life, I felt like I was swimming against the current. When I met Ivy, I was finally paddling in the right direction. And now? Now, I let the flow carry me away. This is happiness, right here.

The dogs bark and come scampering around us, probably wondering why we're so quiet and lying in the snow.

Ivy laughs as Bandit licks her face. "Yes, you too."

That makes me laugh. Again, something I didn't do much of before I met Ivy. "Are you sure about *them*, though? I know I'm a catch and all. But twenty Siberian husky monsters is an entirely different beast. Pun intended."

She giggles again, Bandit still clambering all over her. "Of course. I'll take all of you. You're my family."

And that simple sentence is enough to catapult me into heaven. As I draw her into another addictive kiss, I can't believe how lucky I am to have found Ivy. We lived on different sides of the country, and on the surface, we didn't seem to have anything in common. Not to mention the weird and awkward circumstances in which we met. But all these unexpected turns of events eventually led us to this moment, right here, and all the treasured moments we'll have for the rest of our lives. It led to each of us finding our missing piece.

Serendipity.

Do you want a sneak peek into Zane and Ivy's happily ever after?

Subscribe to my newsletter and read the extended epilogue now!

Ready for spring?

I feel you! I can't wait for the temperatures to go up and all the pretty flowers to bloom!

And next year, we're going to Chicago with Zane's sister, Daisy for a secret identity office romcom!

Preorder Lilies, Lies & Love with 20% off!

Also By Marion De Ré

All the books in the Season of Love series:

Paris, Pumpkins & Puns

Ski, Sparks & Serendipity

Lilies, Lies & Love

To find the complete list of books by Marion De Ré:

If you want help finding your next favorite books, try the <u>TBR Generator</u>!

Acknowledgements

I loved writing this book so much. It reminded me of the winter vacation we used to take as a family when I was young and it was so fun to immerse myself back into this world. Of course, there's a lot more people behind the scenes and I want to thank each and everyone of them.

As always, the first person I want to thank is **Brooke**, my awesome editor. Thank you so much for helping me make this book the best it could be and for all your support.

A big thanks to **Allie**, my amazing beta reader, for all your tremendous help.

Meghan, thank you for proofreading it with your eagle eyes.

Thank you to the talented **Noria** for designing this pretty cover.

Cathy, thank you so much for everything you do on a daily basis You're the best.

To my fantastic **Advanced Readers**, thank you for helping me with typos and for early reviews that stop me from freaking out. I appreciate all of you.

Thank you to Yvette, Melissa, Patty, Katie, Amanda, Devika, Brittany, and Tammy, the members of my Sparkling Street Team for spreading the word about me and my books every day. I feel so blessed to have you on my team.

To the **Bookstagram community**. I'm so grateful for every share, posts and reviews. I love being part of this community. Thank you for making it so special.

Etienne, my husband, thank you for loving me the way you do.

A mes **parents**, merci de m'avoir transmis la passion du ski et pour toutes ces bons souvenirs en vacance à la montagne.

And to my **readers**, you guys are the absolute best. Thank you for each message, purchase, review. I'm the luckiest girl in the world doing the most amazing job, and this is all thanks to you.

About the Author

Marion De Ré is a French national with an American heart. She lives in the French countryside with her husband, Etienne, and her cat, Caline. Growing up with books and being passionate about the English language, she naturally started to write stories in English. You can expect all your beloved tropes in her writing as well as a good dose of humor, and all the feels. When she's not reading or writing, you can find her on a plane to a far-away destination or in a Champagne cellar, indulging in a tasting of her favorite drink.

Marion loves hearing from her readers. Visit her website and sign up for her newsletter to be the first to know about her upcoming books and for exclusive content.

You can also find her on social media:

Facebook and Instagram: @marionderewrites

If you need help finding your favorite book, the TBR Generator is here to help:

Find all links

Connect with Marion

Milton Keynes UK
Ingram Content Group UK Ltd.
UKHW040357111224
452348UK00004B/246